T0082951

THE HOUSE ON
666
SHADOW LANE

CHUCK HUGHES

 iUniverse®

THE HOUSE ON 666 SHADOW LANE

iUniverse books may be ordered through booksellers or by contacting:

iUniverse
1663 Liberty Drive
Bloomington, IN 47403
www.iuniverse.com
844-349-9409

ISBN: 978-1-6632-3412-4 (sc)
ISBN: 978-1-6632-3413-1 (e)

Library of Congress Control Number: 2021925695

Print information available on the last page.

iUniverse rev. date: 01/25/2022

CHAPTER I

FOR A HUNDRED YEARS, THE HOUSE STOOD PROUD, harboring devoted families like the Jones, the Smiths, the Carsons, the Marshals, the, and dozens of other proud owners who called it home. Lawns mowed to perfection while summer pampered gardens of roses, dahlias, azaleas, violets added to the house's pride.

Overnight, pride turned to shame. Sunny days that once brought friendly shadows now brought darkness and repugnance. Green lawns turned brown, elegant flowers faded, shriveled, and died. Tall maple tree limbs that once danced in the wind showing their wealth of green leaves began to wither while dripping blood replaced the sugars and salts that once circulated in the tree's vascular system. Now lifeless, the limbs morphed into tortuous, deformed hand twisted fingers. It seemed *The House* in Savannah knew *HE* was coming.

*　　*　　*

Tallmadge, Ohio

Despite the trivial income from the Millfield Creek Coal Company, twenty-year-old, tall, dark, and lean, Michael

Barlow barely managed to pay apartment rent and put food on the table. Like his back strain, poverty was painful, something he inherited from his father, James Barlow, who knew nothing but the pain of poverty since WW1 and the recession that followed.

Deprivation followed James and his wife through the two decades, with their only glitter of light being the birth of their first son, Michael

.

*   *   *

Tired after finishing his shift in the coal mine, Michael pulled his wool scarf over his face to keep off the stinging-cold October wind. As he passed Davis's Flower Shop, he stopped and looked through the window at the shelves filled with flowers. "Flowers would sure brighten up her day," Michael muttered and reached into his pocket to see how much money he had and pulled out two one-dollar bills, a few nickels, and fewer dimes. Sadly, he reconsidered and passed by the flower shop. A few steps later, he stopped again and recounted the money. The two dollars, sixty cents had not changed, but it was still enough for flowers *if* he skipped lunch for the rest of the week. Flowers for his wife who was carrying his child or a few days without lunch at work? It took him only seconds to make his decision.

Michael climbed the steps to the second-story apartment and walked to the hall's end. Holding the flowers behind his back, he knocked on his door. Hearing the knock, Ellen glanced at the small alarm clock on the small table. It wasn't like her husband to be late coming home. With caution, she looked through the door's small glass hole. Opening the door, she shook her head, "Lost your keys again?"

"Not this time," he said as he handed the bouquet of carnations and peonies to her. "I just wanted to surprise my mother-to-be."

"Michael, you shouldn't have-"

"No *shouldn't have's*. You deserve this."

Ellen answered with a hard hug and a kiss. "Okay, I'll forgive you this time," she said. Michael massaged her bulging belly. Laughing, Ellen pulled his hand away. "Keep that dirty hand off my child until you clean up. And hurry, dinner is almost ready."

"And what great meal has my mother to be whipped up?"

Before she could answer, she grabbed her stomach then bent over. A deep sigh and a loud grimace followed. "It might be . . . be time . . ."

Michael was startled. The baby wasn't due to come for another two months. Once he regained his composure, he walked her to their neatly made-up bed. "Lay down, honey, be calm . . . take deep breaths while I-"

Ellen began laughing once on the bed and wrapped her arms around Michael's neck. "Just kidding, old man," she said. "Teach you to be late for dinner."

When Michael got up, Ellen wasn't sure if he was

3

frightened or angry. The look on his face told her it was both. "Sorry, honey. I shouldn't have done that," she said as she lifted herself off the bed.

"It's okay. You got me that time, but don't do it again. I worry enough about this baby thing as it is. Now, what have you cooked up?"

"Your favorite! Fresh beef and gravy," Ellen said as she straightened her ketchup-stained apron. "And if I don't cut the burner down, it will be burnt fresh beef and gravy,"

Michael raised an eyebrow as he massaged his hands with a bar of soap. The only meat they had, if they had any, was Jacksonville hot dogs. But he never complained since Ellen had a dozen different ways to make hot dogs taste like something other than what they were. "What's so special that we're having beef?"

"Just you being you is reason enough to indulge in a decent meal once in a while."

CHAPTER II

MICHAEL'S HEALTH DETERIORATED LIKE MANY OTHERS who spent years in the coal mine. His shallow breathing, chest tightness, and coughing got worse every year. When his cough began bringing up bloody sputum, he could no longer ignore his failing health.

"It's called black lung disease," he told Ellen when he came home one day after twelve hours in the mine. "Other than getting away from what causes it, there's not much can be done about it."

"You can stop smoking, honey. That might help," Ellen said.

Michael nodded as he looked at the cigarette he was holding in his hand. "You're right." Then he squeezed the pack of Camels and tossed them in the trash.

"Good!" Ellen said as she rewarded him with a hug. "Then you need to find another job somewhere." Seeing the drawn look on Michael's face, she continued. "I know the mine is the only job you ever had, honey, and I know it's part of you, *literally* a part of you, but-"

Each bloody cough told him his wife was right.

"Keeping you from being a widow and my son robbed of a father is more important than any job," he said as he took a deep breath. "But if you don't work in the mine, own the mine, or own a business that supports the mine, finding another job here is not going to happen. But I'll start looking."

Night after night, Michael plowed through the Tallmadge Express's classified section. Other than pleas for mineworkers, the few jobs available were beyond his education. Just as he was beginning to accept his fate, his luck changed. On page two of the section, almost hidden by the dozen advertisements to *buy now* ads, was *Truck drivers needed. Good pay, good benefits, will train if willing to move if needed.* Jotting down the ad's contact number, he rushed to the telephone booth at the corner of the street.

After several minutes of hearing *your time is up* and *please insert another dime*, the interview quickly turned into a new job.

Changing his coal miner's job from days to nights wasn't difficult. It also gave him time to train for his next job. One month later, Michael Barlow was driving for *Nation-Wide Freight Haulers.* The Barlow family's lives were about to change.

Michael worked with Nation-Wide for only two months when he returned from a three-day trip delivering building supplies in Virginia. Dead tired, he pulled his chair up to the dinner table of brazened pork chops, something they could never afford until recently. He took Ellen's hand then thanked her for their meal. Before cutting into the pork chops Closing his eyes, he retook Ellen's hand and said, "Honey, there's something I need to tell you."

"Not bad news, I hope," Ellen said with a half-grin.

Michael returned her smile. "Depends on how you look at it." He waited for her response, but she kept quiet. "We need to get out of this apartment, out of this city, even out of this state."

Ellen's smile vanished into a look of anxiety. "Are we being evicted? Did you lose your job? Did-"

Michael laughed. "No! No! Nothing like that. It's just the opposite. The company is moving some of its drivers to Georgia,

Since most of them wanted to stay here, the boss asked me if I would move. I told him I'd have to talk to my wife about it. He wants me to let him know in a day or two."

Ellen looked around her two-room apartment. A daytime couch during the day, a bed that opened at night, and a small under-stuffed chair pressed between the sofa and radio filled most of the space on one side of the room. A two-burner stove under the only window, and a sink, filled the other side. Behind a door at the end of the room were a small bedroom, a closet, and the only bathroom. "Leaving this place?" Ellen shouted. "You tell him first thing Monday, YES!"

*   *   *

"We're going to miss you here," Nation-Wide's foreman, Edward Johnson, said when Michael agreed to move. "But I think you're doing the right thing. Georgia's a good place to be. We can give you a week off with pay to make a move to

Savanna. Another benefit is the housing. The company has a few houses they *rent to own* to the employees at a pretty low price." Handing him a card, he continued. "Get in touch with this lady when you get there. She handles the housing stuff."

It only took a day for the movers to load up the meager pieces of furniture and personal items they wanted to take with them. After the last box was packed, Michael looked back at the place they had called home for many years.

"Are you sad about leaving?" Ellen asked.

Michael wiped his eyes with his sleeve. "Kinda. We've had so many good times here and so many friends, that-" He paused as he watched the puzzled look on Ellen's face, then laughed. "Gotcha!" Now we're even with that *baby's coming* thing."

Ellen swatted him on his head. "Sarcasm doesn't fit you, so don't give me that *poor me* look. They left Tallmadge's dirty smell and blight a week later and began their trip to Savannah and a new life.

*   *   *

After several rest area stops and a night at a motel in Charlotte, NC, they arrived at the real estate company's office as his boss told him to do. Mary Ann. Jacob was there to greet them. "I hope your drive was pleasant," the tall, thin woman said. Her southern draw was evidence that she was either Georgia born or planted there years ago.

"Yes, it was a comfortable trip," Michael said as he took Ellen's hand. "And this is my wife, Ellen."

Ellen rubbed her bulging belly. "And him, or her. Not sure about a name yet, but we're working on it."

"Good to meet you," Mary Ann said. "The movers called me as soon as they arrived asking where they should deliver your things. I gave them your new address, so they'll meet you there tomorrow morning to offload your things. I figured you would be tired, so I reserved a room for you at the Franklin lodge for the night. But I think you're hungry. Let me introduce you to one of Savannah's most popular meals. You'll love any one of them."

Michael thought Shrimp and Grits were more a manly dish than the Fried Green Tomatoes Ellen decided on. After eating at a restaurant for the first time in years, Mary Ann took them back to the lodge. "I'll pick you up in the morning and take you to your new home."

Once they checked in at the lodge, a young man dressed in a fancy uniform and a blue cap picked up their two suitcases. "I'll get them," Michael said.

The young man looked surprised. "It's okay, sir, but this is my pleasure."

The room was almost as large as the entire apartment they left behind. Not being used to such luxury, Michael was surprised when the bellboy just stood there.

Ellen laughed. "Michael, give the man a dollar for his help."

"Thank you, sir," the young man said. "If you need anything, just call the front desk."

After they were alone, Ellen flopped down on the Queen-sized bed while Michael pulled up a chair in front of the television, something he could never have afforded in Ohio. "How do you turn this thing on," he muttered as he fiddled with the television dials.

Ellen shook her head and tossed him the remote. "You'd think an intelligent truck driver like you would know how to push buttons on things."

"Hey, this thing works," Michael said mockingly.

After watching Seinfeld for the first time, sleep overcame him. The next thing he heard was a telephone ringing. He looked at the clock on the side table. "Damn, it's nine o'clock." Almost knocking the phone off the table, he grabbed the phone. "Hello."

"This is Mary Ann. I'll wait for you folks down here in the lodge."

While Michael showered and shaved, Ellen was dressing. While she was finishing cleaning up, Michael met with Mary Ann. "Sorry, but we overslept," he said. "Ellen will be here in a few minutes."

"That's okay. We have plenty of time. You have breakfast yet?"

"No, but Ellen will need to eat. I get by with just a good night's sleep, but she needs breakfast, or she gets cranky.

"We can stop by the pancake place if you want, Mary Ann suggested."

"Thanks. Give me the directions, and we'll meet you there."

"No need to take two cars. We'll take mine if it's okay." After a long pause, she came closer to Michael. "Now that I have you alone, Mister Barlow, there is something I need to tell you about the house you're moving into." Whispering, she continued. "It might not be important to you, but since you'll be living there, I think you need to know."

"Should I be scared?" Michael asked.

"No, not really, but it might upset your wife, so just keep it between us." Mary Ann looked over her shoulder at the stairway to make sure Ellen hadn't come down yet. "The original owners built the house sometime in the nineteen hundreds. After they passed it on to their children, they passed it on to their children, and so on. But-"

"It's an old house!" Michael interrupted. "Is that what you're trying to tell me?"

Mary Ann paused, then smiled. "Not just that."

"We don't mind an old house. They have their own historical stories. Besides, an old house is about all we can afford."

"Well, this one is affordable, that's for sure. Anyway, the company bought it and kept it up along with the other houses they own." When she saw Ellen jogging to them, she said, "Just forget what I said. I think you'll like the house."

"Sorry, I'm so late, but I had to finish my coffee," Ellen said after taking a deep breath. "I can't get through the morning without it, but I sure can use something to eat."

After a plate of pancakes smothered with butter and maple syrup, and a second cup of coffee, the Barlows headed towards their new neighborhood

After fifteen minutes, lecturing the Barlows on Georgian's do's and don'ts while pointing out places of interest, Mary Ann took a left turn. "This is Shadow Lane," she said.

"Kinda funny name," Ellen said.

"Yes, it is," Mary Ann said. "But it's named after the shade it gets from all of these tall maple trees. You might not see the sun a lot, but you know it's there. You know, no sun, no shadows," she said with a laugh. As they continued, they passed homes on both sides of the road, some small but well-attended, some in need of care, and three large mansion-style houses. "Most of the folks here are just middle class, but-"

"Middle class?" Michael repeated with a hint of irritation.

"Not that there's anything wrong with being middle class," Mary Ann added when she noticed Michael's tone. "I just meant there are a few rich families here too. Most inherited their money. Some came from hard work. Mister Swartz is a good example. He worked for a while with the owner of the local funeral home. He saved his money and learned the skill, or whatever morticians need to know, and bought the business when the owner died. There were a lot of jokes going around, you know, about one mortician fixing up another mortician."

Suddenly the street had only a few houses. Noticing this, Ellen broke the few quiet minutes that followed. "There doesn't seem to be many houses on this street," she said as she looked out the window.

"There used to be a lot of houses here too, but over time they just decayed and were torn down . . . your house is just around the corner up ahead. The good part is you don't have only a few neighbors to bother you."

"I don't mind neighbors," Ellen said. They can often be helpful."

"There's Sam's grocery store," Mary Ann said as she pointed to a small one-level building. Sam has about everything you might need. They charge a bit more than the larger stores, but they're convenient. There's a Shell gas station further up the road. They have a lot of things besides gas if you don't mind their prices."

Suddenly, Mary Ann slowed down and pulled into a narrow driveway.

Ellen's frown and the shaking of her head made it clear that the two-story house was not what she expected. The first thing she noticed was the twisted, leafless tree limbs that seemed more guarding than welcoming. Then she decided that tree leaves would hide the house from the harsh heat of Georgia summers. Next, she looked at the house itself. Aged grey paint was peeling away. A porch swing rested in front of a smudged window on one side of a double door. Another window on the other side of the doors was just as dirty. The peaked second floor had only one narrow window. "Not much room up there."

"It's small but a little bigger than it looks from down here," Mary Ann said. "There's enough room for a small bedroom or maybe an office."

Michael looked at his wife, then at Mary Ann. "Ellen's right," he said. "Whoever lived here didn't take care of the house."

"They moved out recently," Mary Ann explained. "I think it had to do with some family problems, but it won't take much to get the outside back in shape and the inside cleaned. I believe there's some new furniture too."

Then Michael noticed the house number hanging on one of the posts holding the peaked second floor. "Is 999 the house number?"

"No, it must have fallen and put back upside down," she said as she turned the numbers back up. "There, that's fixed."

"666 Shady Lane? Kinda' spooky!" Michael said with a laugh.

Mary Ann just raised her shoulders and smiled. "Let's take a tour of the inside, okay?"

The inside of the house was just as unkempt as the outside. The only thing Ellen liked was the wooden living room floor that was larger than the two-room house they left in Tallmadge. She closed her eyes and took a deep breath when she saw the living room's green-leaf wallpaper clinging to the living room into the narrow hall's windowless back door.

A large, wire-screen-caged fireplace took up part of the room on one side of the room. A pile of plastic wood rested on one side of it as if the fireplace was ready to heat a room that seemed not to need heat.

At first sight of the fireplace, Ellen pictured sitting in front of a crackling fire during a cold winter night. The picture faded when she realized this was not Ohio

Michael saw her look of disappointment. "I know, honey, it needs some work too, but it's something I can take care of."

Mary Ann saw Ellen looking at the fireplace. "It's almost summer all year round down here," she said. "Other than having it for decoration, you're not likely to need that." Then Mary Ann continued Ellen her tour.

On the other side of a door, the dining room opened into a kitchen with a small table, four chairs, upper wall cabinets, a refrigerator, and what looked like a new gas stove. "It's just big enough," Ellen whispered to Michael. Another door led to two a hallway and two bedrooms and a curving stairway leading to the only second-floor room. The room's ceiling was just as it looked from outside, small, and peaked like a tent.

"It'll be good for storage. Maybe a good place for Andrew to play," Michael replied. Then he started towards the narrow steps.

"Where're you going?" Ellen asked.

"I'll be right back. I'm going out back to see what's in the shed out back."

Ellen shook her head. "A typical Michael Barlow treasure hunt, she muttered with a grin. Then she called to Michael, "Michael, people don't leave treasures behind when they move."

"You never know. Ellen." Michael said as he laughed and started down the steps. "People often move and leave things they call junk behind them, but to others are-"

"Treasures! Yes, I know, people like you," Ellen jabbered.

"You forget the things we left behind when we left Ohio."

Ellen looked at Mary Ann and shook her head. "What we left in the old house in Ohio were three faded, cheap pictures of people we didn't even know hanging on the wall. He called them *works of art.*"

Michael's treasures consisted of a wooden box of garden tools, several rusted shovels, a broken rake, a wheelbarrow with one stand missing, an old kitchen sink, and pieces of nineteen-forty car parts filled the small building. That didn't bother him. After all, that was what sheds were for, dumping things you don't need or might need one day. What did trouble him was the graveyard just a shout away from the house. "Ellen's not going to like this," he muttered. He decided not to mention it, at least not on the first day.

Once back at the house, he called out to Ellen. "Where are you, honey?"

"She's up here with me," Mary Ann answered.

"What's the upstairs look like?" Michael asked.

"Just wasted space," Ellen said as she followed Mary Ann down the narrow stairs. "Not good for more than storage."

When Michael saw the truck pulling into the driveway, he decided not to mention the graveyard. Instead, he shouted again. "The movers are here." Michael took her hand and helped her down the narrow steps. "Why don't you stay here and supervise while I go back with Mary Ann to pick up our car? And while I'm gone, you stay away from those stairs."

"I can manage steps," Ellen replied. I don't-"

"I know you can, honey," Michael said with a mocking smile as he helped her off the last step. "I just want to be here to catch you if you do fall."

Ellen was cleaning the door's window while Michael was gone, and the movers had everything when there was a knock on the door. She hesitated. Michael wasn't gone long enough to be back. As she swiped the smudge off one of the window panes, there was another knock, this time a lot harder. "Just a minute," she said.

When she opened the door, she saw an overdressed-for-the-weather, short, heavy woman with an umbrella in one hand and an overloaded purse in the other.

"I'm Olivia Collins," the woman said as she folded her unnecessary umbrella to free a hand to point at a house several dozen yards away. "I live over there, so I thought I'd come over and say hello to you all. I'm just a friendly neighbor. Not that many 'round here to do it. So welcome to Shadow Lane."

"That's very nice of you, Mrs. Collins. I'm Ellen Barlow, and my husband's name is Michael. He's running errands now. I'd invite you in, but my house is in a mess."

"No matter, Miss Ellen," the lady said as she stretched her neck to look over Ellen's shoulder into her house. "I don't mind, and I surely won't stay long."

"Well, just ignore the mess," Ellen said as she led the woman into the living room. "I'd offer you something to drink, but we're just getting settled in, and I don't know where anything is yet."

"No matter," the woman said as she looked at the bulge in Ellen's dress. "How far are you?"

"How far? Oh, you mean how far my pregnant is?" Ellen hesitated as if she wasn't sure. "Hmm, about eight months, so I should be delivering a month from now."

Mrs. Collins shook her head. "A month! Maybe, but don't be surprised if it comes sooner. I've delivered a lot of babies in my years, and I can usually tell up to the day. It looks like it'll be a boy too."

Ellen narrowed her eyes. "A boy? How can you tell?"

"My goodness, child, if I know about anything, I know about these things."

"Are you a doctor?"

"Now, do I look like a doctor?" After a wide grin, she snickered. "Okay, I can't tell, I just guess. Half the time, I'm right, half the time I'm wrong."

CHAPTER III

I<small>T TOOK</small> M<small>ICHAEL AND</small> E<small>LLEN ONLY A WEEK TO SETTLE IN</small> and for Michael to go back on the road again. While he was away, Mrs. Collins made daily visits with Ellen. The sixty-five-year-old widow next door served as the daily news and at times made the daily news for the few families living on the upper end of Shadow Lane. She was the closest thing to a doctor within miles. Between gossiping and delivering babies, life ear-dropping filled her life.

On her next visit with Ellen, Mrs. Collins spilled her history. "I lived here with my husband most of my life. Then Mister Collins caught cancer and died, leaving me alone with my blonde-haired daughter."

"You have a daughter? How old is she."

"Her name's Rachel. She's 'bought eighteen now."

"Rachel? That's a nice name. So you're not alone."

"Might as well be, she's not here that much, but that's okay. Nowadays, kids have places to go and people to see."

A week later, while she was knitting a jacket for her cat, Mrs. Collins heard a knocking on her door. "I know, Melissa, just when you get comfortable, someone comes knocking. Rachel, answer the door, will you? I'm pretty busy right now." While waiting for Rachel to answer, there was another pounding. Mrs. Collins took a deep breath, grabbed her wooden cane, and slowly pushed herself up from her couch. "That's okay, Rachel, I got it."

When she opened the door, she was surprised to see Michael since he rarely spoke to her other than to say *hello* or a *how're you*. When she saw his taut look, she knew it wasn't a social call.

"Mrs. Collins, it's Ellen . . . I just got home from work. I think she's ready to have the baby. Can you help us?"

Then, Mrs. Collins shook her head and grabbed a black bag and a handful of small towels. "My gosh, Mister Barlow, you men put the children in there, then you want someone else to pull them out. Good thing we women know how to do things, but she picked a poor day to have a baby, you know it being Halloween and all. But it don't matter none 'cause nobody comes to trick or treat up this part of the street anyway. They just go up to the rich folk's houses. Better treats, I guess. Anyway, it's as good a day as any to have a baby. By the way, do you know that Mexican man in the brown house next to me?" After making sure Michael knew how bad her neighbor was and what she knew about him, Mrs. Collins hesitated and closed her eyes. "He's been up to no good again."

Michael shook his head and grabbed her arm. "No, I don't know him."

"David Ricardo! That's his name, David Ricardo. Why everyone knows that old man." Again, her eyes closed as she shook her head. "I worry about Rachel being around when he's about, and I feel sorry for that little boy he has, but-"

"Please hurry, Mrs. Collins."

"No need to hurry. It'll come out when it's ready, whether we're there or not. But about Mister Ricardo," she hesitated as she looked around to make sure no one else would hear her, "now you can't tell anyone about this, but-"

Michael pulled her towards his apartment. "Please! Ellen's in labor. You can tell me about Mister Ricardo later."

Ellen was sweating and panting when Mrs. Collins arrived. "Hang in there, Ellen. Everything's gonna be okay now that I'm here."

After twenty minutes of severe pain and Mrs. Collins' loud coaching, a baby was pushing its way out of the birth canal into the world, but with legs first followed by a pointed head. "Oh my God, it's a breech birth," Mrs. Collins muttered. Never having to deliver a breech, she wasn't sure what to do other than to pull gently on the baby's feet. "That's what was causing her so much pain," she whispered to Michael. Ellen's pain began to ease as the baby slipped out into Mrs. Collins' hands. Now that the pain was fading, all Ellen cared about was her baby.

"It's okay, Ellen," Mrs. Collins said. "And it's a boy . . . a small boy, thank God. Had he been larger, I don't think he would have made it alive." Seeing Michael's confusion, she tried to explain a breech birth. "Babies are supposed to come out head first, but sometimes they don't. That delays the delivery, and the baby can suffocate before it's born." As she cut the umbilical cord, something else dripped out of Ellen's body. Seeing it, she froze and made the sign of the cross. "Did you know she was having twins . . . at least what should have been two babies?"

Michael grimaced. "What do you mean, two babies?"

Wanting to avoid explaining what she saw, the self-taught midwife ignored Michael's question, wiped the baby's face, forced a smile, and handed him to Ellen. "Here's your son, Ellen. What are you going to name him?"

Cuddling the newborn child, Ellen sighed and looked at her husband. "We decided to name him after his father. He'll be Michael Andrew Barlow, but I don't want both of them to come running when I shout out *Michael*, so we'll call him Andrew."

"Andrew's a good, strong name," Mrs. Collins said as she cleaned Ellen as much as a wet rag would let her, and then she looked back at the fetus remnant that should have been a baby. Shaking her head, she looked up at Michael. Her foreboding look told him something shocked her, and it wasn't the breech delivery. It was something she didn't want Ellen to know.

"Mister Barlow, your wife's been through a lot," she continued as she made eye contact with Michael. "Why don't you take me back to my house and let your wife rest for a while."

Once they were in the hall, Michael put his hands on

the trembling woman's shoulders. Looking into her eyes, he asked, "I don't understand. What did you see in there?"

"Not much to understand," she said as they crossed the dying grass. "Most of the time, there's no problem delivering a baby. Not even twins if both are-" she hesitated for a minute then continued. "If both are fully developed." Pointing her finger at Michael, she continued. "But telling your wife about it won't change anything, so there's no need for her to grieve over something she had no control over."

"You're probably right, but-"

"I'm usually right, Mister Barlow," the slow-walking woman said as she wiped her thick glasses with her apron. "Just don't let what you saw in there ruin your life or her life. If I was you, I'd just forget about it and be happy with the boy you do have. Other than being a bit small, he seems to be okay."

"I know, but since *it* . . . *he* contributed to the survival of the baby we do have, he deserves to have a name too."

"I think that would be a big mistake, Mister Barlow, and it's not likely you'll get the church to hold a funeral. Maybe a preacher's blessing at best," Mrs. Collins said. "Anyway, let me ask my preacher, Pastor Garland. He might be able to give you some advice."

Michael ignored the agitation in her tone. "Maybe we'll name him after my father, Jimm Barlow. And we should have a ceremony, something enough to recognize him and bury him like you'd do anyone else."

"Then you gonna have to tell her," Mrs. Collins muttered, "I don't know how she's gonna take it, so it might be best to have Pastor Garland be with you when you do tell her."

Michael closed his eyes and shook his head. "I don't know either, but my wife's pretty strong, and someone else being there would only make things worse. Anyway, she will need to know if we have a funeral. I think she'll want one too. I'll think about it, though. For now, I just want to see my baby and thank you for all you did."

"Wasn't much at all, but I still think you need to just put this behind you, but I guess it ain't none of my business. Anyway, I'll have Pastor Garland talk to you. He's pretty good at it. Now I have to get back home. My Rachel will be home soon. I always have his dinner on the table for her. Like all kids, she eats then goes out with her friends. I don't see her for weeks at a time. She hardly comes by anymore, but she's usually busy."

Michael dreaded going home and telling his wife what he had decided. When he reached his house, he sat down on the porch swing instead of going in as if a few minutes of thought would clear his mind and change the unchangeable. *What to say and how to say it* ran through his mind. *I guess it's better to be happy with what we have.* He closed his eyes and ran his palms down his face. His emotions smothered him with visions of a half-born thing that would never be a child.

As tears ran down his cheek, he opened the door and went in to do what he had to do.

*   *   *

It was Sunday. The remains of Jimm Barlow were still at the funeral home in the large cremation jar while Swartz was waiting to hear what they wanted to do with the *thing*. Ellen was breastfeeding while Michael stood at the bedroom door quietly listening to her soft voice singing to their baby, her newly born son. Ellen lifted Andrew over her shoulder when her song ended and gently padded his back. The result was a gentle burp followed by a brief cry. "That's a good boy," Ellen said as she rocked back and forth until the crying stopped.

Michael hesitated to go into the room. He didn't want to spoil the moment his wife had waited for over the eight years of their marriage. Discussing *almost babies* and funerals would undoubtedly do just that. *But there won't ever be a good time,* he said to himself. He let her know he was there only after laying her son down in the baby's crib. "Looks like you mastered motherhood without any problem," he said as he hugged Ellen then leaned over the crib to look at his son.

"I took the job the moment I saw him," she said as she looked over Michael's shoulder at the baby. "He looks a lot like you."

Michael laughed. "Hope he's not that unlucky, but thanks for the compliment anyway."

"You know you're good-looking," Ellen said, "so don't try to sound so modest."

"Well, I try to keep that a secret just between us."

"Go ahead and pick him up. I know you want to."

"He's sleeping now, so let him rest. Speaking of rest, how are you doing?"

"Okay, but while we're talking about *speaking,* what were you and Mrs. Collins talking about when I was in so much pain delivering our baby?"

Still struggling with what he had to say and not knowing how to say it, he backed away from the crib. "Considering the pain you were having, how would you know if we said anything?"

"Michael, I can walk and chew gum at the same time. I caught the look on her face and your response. So, no secrets, okay? What went wrong?"

Michael took a deep breath and sat down next to his wife. "Okay, Mrs. Collins did tell me something. She also said that telling you would not change anything, so I decided to wait until the right time came, but I knew there would never be a right time."

Ellen sat down on the bed. "Michael, the right time has come!"

Searching for words that would make the horrible sound less horrible, Michael told her what Mrs. Collins said and what he saw.

Ellen closed her eyes and shook her head. "I don't know

what I did wrong, but I'm so sorry I robbed you of being a father of twins," Ellen said as she picked Andrew up again.

"You didn't do anything wrong, honey, not anything. Mrs. Collins said these things just happen, not often, but sometimes they just happen, and there's nothing anybody can do about it."

"What are we supposed to do," Ellen muttered as she held back her tears, "just flush it down the toilet?"

"No," Michael said as he lifted Ellen's chin and looked into her watery eyes. "Whatever state it . . . *he* was in, he was our child, and he deserves to be treated with respect." Then there was a knock on the door.

"I'll get it," Michael said. "It's probably Mrs. Collins again."

When Michael opened the door, Ellen could hear him talking, then the voice she listened to every Sunday made its way into the bedroom. "Ellen, it's me, Mrs. Collins, and Pastor Garland."

Ellen closed her eyes in frustration as she put Andrew back down. Although she was in no mood to see anyone after what she had just learned from her husband, she pulled her robe around her and patted her red eyes with a napkin. "Have them set down in the living room. I'll be there in a minute."

Bible in hand, Pastor Garland stood up when Ellen came in. "Sorry to disturb you, Mrs. Barlow, but Mrs. Collins told me about your . . . concern . . . about the baby, I mean. The one that-"

"The one that didn't make it," Mrs. Collins said as she took Ellen's hand.

"Mrs. Collins told me you might want to hold a ceremony and bury the *remains*, but-"

Ellen interrupted the preacher. "He's more than remains. He was a son and-"

Seeing the pain in Ellen's face, Michael spoke up. "My wife and I want you to treat our *child* like you would any other dead child. That includes a funeral."

The Pastor opened his bible. "Romans 14:8. *If we live, we live for the Lord. So, whether we live or die, we belong to the Lord.*" He looked at Mrs. Collins, then at Ellen and Michael. "This thing was not born alive, so it doesn't have a soul; it doesn't *belong* to God."

"How dare you bring God into this!"

Ellen's angry tone surprised Michael. It also sent a message to the pastor saying he had gone too far. All the preacher could say was, "I'm sorry I said that, but I haven't been in a situation like this before . . . I may have phrased my belief wrong. Forgive me. Can I at least pray for you?"

Ellen answered with a glare. "Yes, Pastor! You do that!"

Michael, Ellen, Mrs. Collins, and baby Andrew were the only ones present when they buried Jimm Barlow II in the cemetery behind 666 Shadow Lane.

CHAPTER IV

Eight years of birthdays and Halloweens passed with the Barlows living on Shadow Lane. They celebrated Andrew's birthday every October thirty-first, then they visited their son, Jimm, resting in the cemetery on the hill.

Although Halloween came on a Thursday, Michael took the day off to go to the cemetery every October 31st. Once they were there, Andrew pulled away from his mother's hand and ran up to the granite stones. While he played, Michael and Ellen knelt in front of Jimm's memorial plate. Wiping away her tears, Ellen read the words engraved in the granite plate:

JIMM BARLOW II
OCTOBER 31 1994 TO OCTOBER 31 1994
HE GAVE HIS LIFE FOR HIS BROTHER
MAY HE REST IN PEACE

"I know coming up here even once a year hurts," Ellen said as she held her husband's hand, "but I can't forget him any more than I could forget Andrew." After a brief prayer, she called Andrew and told him it was time to go.

"I'll be there in a minute," Andrew said as he dodged from one granite stone to another, stopping only long enough to peek out from behind each other and shouting, "You can't catch me."

"Andrew, we're going home now," Michael said. "Get your butt down here." When Andrew caught up with them, Michael took his hand. "Who were you talking to up there?"

"Just my friend. He likes playing touch tag."

Ellen took his other hand and asked, "I didn't see anyone there. What's his name?"

"He don't have a name, and it's hard to see him he's so fast. But I'm the fastest, and I always win. Sometimes he gets mad at me when I win and tells me to go back to Ohio where I belong."

Michael laughed and looked at him. "Doesn't sound like a good friend to me."

Andrew ran the rest of the way to the house, leaving his parents strolling behind him. Ellen gave Michael a sad look and sighed. "It's not funny, Michael; it's sad."

"Sad?" Michael Jabbered.

"Don't laugh, Michael. It is sad!" Ellen sobbed. "It's sad he only has make-believe friends to play with."

"Sorry, I shouldn't have laughed," Michael murmured. "Do you think Mrs. Collins could introduce you to someone who has kids his age? She seems to know everyone on the Lane."

Ellen nodded. "At least he'll have friends when he starts school back to school. But it won't hurt to ask her."

*   *   *

After coming home, Michael and Ellen played their year-old game of ignoring it being Andrew's birthday. Finally, Andrew brought it up. "Dad, do you know what today is?"

"You want to play a guessing game? Okay, I'll play," Michael said as he closed his eyes and put a finger to his chin. "What is today? Let me guess; Hmm, Christmas? No! That's not for a couple of months. Maybe Easter."

"I haven't seen any Easter Bunnies jumping around, so it can't be Easter either," Andrew said with a deep laugh. Another hmm. "I know, Dad. It's Halloween and my birthday. I'm eight years old now."

Michael lifted the boy in the air. After putting him back on the living room floor, he pulled out several packages from behind the couch, all wrapped in bright red and blue paper, and handed them to Andrew. "Did you think we would forget your birthday, little guy?"

"No, you never forget. Can I open them now?"

"Blow out the candles first," Ellen said after she set the homemade cake with seven glowing candles on the table.

After blowing out the candles, Andrew tossed the wrapping paper across the room. He did the same with the socks, the jeans, and a Mickey Mouse shirt. Then he tore into the remaining two boxes. "A fire truck! Does it have a whistle?"

Michael sat on the floor next to his son. "It's called a siren, and yes, it has one. Just push this button."

He ran the fire truck around the floor for a few minutes, then opened the next neatly wrapped present. "Wow!" he shouted. "A gun!"

"It's a nerf gun, son," Michael said as he showed the anxious boy how to load it. "Put this in here, then pull this back, and then pull the trigger."

After loading the gun, Andrew pointed it at his father and sent a sponge ball hitting him in the chest. "Oh, you got me," Michael said as he faked a chest wound then fell on the floor.

Andrew laughed. "I'm a good shooter," he said as he reloaded the gun and aimed at his father again.

Michael ducked this time. "Ha, you missed me."

"You cheated, Dad," Andrew said as he shot another round, hitting Michael in the chest again.

Michael lifted his hands in surrender. "Okay, you win. Besides being your birthday, what else is today?"

"Halloween!" Andrew shouted. "Can we go trick or treating later?"

"Sure. I think Mommy can fix you up some type of costume."

"How about a ghost?" Michael suggested. "All you have to do is punch some holes in a white sheet."

Smiling, Ellen watched the two loves of her life from the couch. Her smile suddenly vanished when she saw a change in Andrew. He was looking at Michael in a way she had never seen before. "What's wrong, Andrew?'

Andrew answered by throwing his new truck against the wall. Ellen jumped to her feet and grabbed him by the arm. "Andrew, don't you ever look at your father like that, and don't treat the presents he gave you that way."

Wide-eyed, Michael picked up the broken truck. "Andrew, what's got into you, boy?"

"Someone broke my fire truck!" Andrew shouted as he looked at his broken present."

"You just did, I don't know why, but you did!" Michael shouted.

Not wanting to show her frustration and ruin Andrew's birthday, Ellen put her hand on Michael's arm. "I'm sure it was an accident, honey. He just misses you, that's all. He'll get over you being gone once he understands it's your job."

"It's okay," Michael said as he sat down on the floor beside Andrew. "Son, I'm a truck driver now. I know you miss me, and I miss you and Mommy when I'm gone, but that's what truck drivers do. I'll always be your dad, and I'll always come back, and I'll always bring you a present like I did last week?"

"What present?"

"You know, the wood boy whose nose gets longer and longer when he tells fibs? I even read you a story about him."

"He's a doll? Dolls are for girls," Andrew said with a frown."

"Well, Andrew, he's not really a doll; he's a puppet. His name is Pinocchio. You remember-"

Andrew suddenly hugged his father. "Yea, I remember 'cause I named him Mister Long Nose. I like him, and I like my truck. Can you fix it, Dad?"

Michael picked up the truck and examined it. "I think I can, but you need to be more careful with your things."

"Thank your father," Ellen said with a sigh as she took Andrew by the hand and led him to the kitchen table. "Let's eat before dinner gets cold, then get ready for trick or treating."

After spending an hour on Shadow Lane, Andrew returned tired with a plastic pumpkin half filled with candy. "I think I scared a lot of people in my ghost costume. Billy Ricardo was dressed like the devil, and he acted like one. He pushed me around and dared me to go with him up to the graveyard. I said no, I have to go home. He pushed me again then laughed at me, and said, *you're just a scared mommy's boy.* I don't like him at all. I wanted to hurt him real bad."

"You don't go around hurting people, Andrew, so just forget about Billy," Ellen said as she helped Andrew out of his costume. "He's just a bully, and most bullies are scared. I bet he has never gone up there, at least not by himself. But you, my scary boy, need to go to bed."

When Saturday morning came and breakfast was over,

Andrew shot nerf balls at everyone again. "Michael, I'm going to see Mrs. Collins for a few minutes. Andrew, do you want to come with me?"

"Can I bring my gun?" he asked as he pointed his new present at her.

"I rather you don't, son. We won't be there long."

*   *   *

Olivia Collins rose with the sun most mornings. Just as the sun had a regular daily routine, she had her's too. After feeding her cat, she would pull her knitting basket out of the closet, move her chair close to the window so she wouldn't miss any happenings from her neighbor in the brown house, then wait on the porch waiting for Mister Jenkins to bring the mail.

Although most of her mail came at the end of the month when one bill or another was due, or some magazine she ordered but never read, Mister Jenkins always stopped long enough to wave at her and say, "Hey, Mrs. Collins, how are you doing. Sorry but there's no mail today." That was her prompt to spend the rest of the day knitting while gossiping over the phone.

As usual, after an hour or two changing loops of yarn into a woolen fabric, she closed her eyes and dozed off. Just as she fell asleep, someone hammering on her door startled her. "Hold on, I'm coming," she shouted as she set her needlework aside and pulled her bedroom robe around her. Looking through the small peephole in the door, she was surprised to see Ellen and Andrew on the porch. "Y'all come on in, Ellen," she said as she opened the door. "Anything wrong?"

"No, no. We just don't see you outside very often anymore."

"It's this arthritis," Mrs. Collins said as she rubbed her neck. "It surely slows me down." However, it wasn't just back pain and arthritis that troubled her; it was her health that had deteriorated over the years since the delivery of Andrew.

"It seems we only see you when we need your help, so you let us know if we can help *you*, And Andrew wanted to give you this," Ellen said as she handed the aging woman a large slice of cake.

"I'm nine years old today," Andrew said with a wide grin.

"Why, thank you, Andrew," Mrs. Collins said as she put the cake on the side table next to her chair. "I do like cake. I'll eat it later when my daughter comes home."

Ellen was surprised. "I didn't know you had any children."

"Why yes, I do, a daughter."

"I've never seen her outside," Andrew said.

"That's because she goes to college and doesn't come around much anymore. You know how it is with an eighteen-year-old! If they're not working, they're out with their friends." Then she shook her head. "Of course, you don't know about teenagers, but you will when your boy here grows up."

Ellen looked at the pictures filling the wall. Most of them

were pictures of a young Mrs. Collins, a man she assumed was Mister Collins, and a baby.

"Those pictures are of my husband and me," Mrs. Collins said as she struggled to reach for one of the dozens of pictures scattered around the table.

"And the baby?"

"That's my Rachel when she was 'bout a year or so. Here, let me show you a better picture of her I took last year."

"She's very pretty, Mrs. Collins," Ellen said as she looked at the picture of a blonde-haired teenager.

"I think she is, but then all parents think their child is pretty."

"Parent or not, you're right, Mrs. Collins," Ellen said as she handed the picture back to her and stood up to leave. "I'm anxious to meet her; what's her name?"

"Rachel. She liked her name so much that she wanted to name her cat after her, but I convinced her to give it another name. I told her Melissa would be a good name for a cat."

While they were chatting, Ellen brought up the topic of families with children Andrew's age. After giving deep thought and running through a dozen families, Mrs. Collins shook her head. "All the folks here have lived here a long time. Most live further down the street, except the Mexican boy next door to me. His name's Billy. He's 'bout your boy's age, maybe seven, maybe eight, but I wouldn't want my child going there.

"His father's a widower. Widow or not, you can't trust

him, you know, being from Mexico and all. But-" The mewling of her cat cut her off as it jumped out of Andrew's hands and ran into the kitchen.

"It's okay, boy," she grunted. "She's a bit shy with people. Go get her if you want."

When the cat's mewling stopped, Ellen called to Andrew, "Let the cat alone. We're ready to go."

"Melissa, Ellen, her name's Melissa," Mrs. Collins repeated, then she shouted to Andrew. "Son, just bring my Melissa back in here." After wiping away tears, she patted Ellen's hand. "Sometimes I think she's my only friend, except you and Mister Barlow, of course. I don't get many visitors. I just don't know why. Guess it's 'cause I'm an old woman."

"Well, we'll try to visit more often." Then Ellen shouted to Andrew again. "Andrew, I said bring the . . . Melissa back in here so we can go."

"I can't find her," the boy replied."

"Then come back in here and tell Mrs. Collins goodbye," Ellen said. "You owe her more than you will ever know."

After the goodbyes were said and the Barlows left, Mrs. Collins called for Melissa. When the cat didn't respond, she hobbled into the kitchen. Melissa wasn't there, so Mrs. Collins looked into the bathroom. What she saw made her heart pound. She grabbed her nitroglycerin and put one under her tongue when her chest pain followed.

* * *

Once they were home, Ellen filled the bathtub for Andrew's bath. "Take off those dirty clothes," she said.

"Just don't look, Mommy, I'm grown up now," Andrew said as he tossed his clothes on the floor and stepped into the bathtub while Ellen waited patiently on the other side of the door.

"Okay, you can come in now, Mommy, " he said to his mother while she was picking up rumbled clothes off the floor.

"You'd expect *a grown-up* boy wouldn't get his clothes so dirty," Ellen teased. After tossing the clothes into the dirty clothes basket, she went back to the bathroom. "Did you hurt yourself playing?"

"No, Mommy," Andrew said.

"Are you sure?"

"I said I didn't, Mommy."

"Well, you've got blood on your new shirt."

"That's where Mrs. Collins' cat scratched me."

The unheard voice giggled. *It won't scratch us anymore.*

An hour after Ellen and Andrew left, two Police Officers arrived at Mrs. Collins' door. One was a stiff, six-footman, the other a shorter, blonde-haired woman.

*   *   *

"I'm Officer Jessica Marten," Marten said, then looked at the other policeman who was a step behind her. "And this is my partner, Officer Richard Williams.

"Was it you who made the 911 call? Williams asked."

Mrs. Collins broke down in tears as she told the officers what she found in her bathroom.

"Was anyone in the house when you found your cat?" Officer Williams asked.

"Melissa, Mister Williams, her name is . . . was Melissa and she was more than a cat--"

"It's Officer Williams, ma'am."

"Whatever," Mrs. Collins mumbled as she put her daily tablets into her mouth. A gulp of the last of her coffee followed.

Trying to curb her partner's curtness, Officer Marten sat down next to Mrs. Collins on the aging couch. "I know how you feel, Mrs. Collins," she said. Not only did the detective's soft tone speak of understanding, but her blonde ponytail and closed-mouth smile were even more comforting. "I have a pet too, a little Shih Tzu," Marten said. I don't have any children, so I spoil her a lot, but-"

Mrs. Collins glared at Officer Williams. "I bet he don't have no pets," she said as she puckered her lips and squinted her eyes."

"I don't think he has one either, but what he was asking was if anyone else was in the apartment besides you when you last saw your cat . . . your Melissa.

"Why didn't he just say that?" Mrs. Collins asked as she looked up at Officer Williams then back at Marten. "But nobody but me. I was the only one here. My daughter was supposed to come, but she didn't show up. I guess she had other things to do, so it was just me.

"But my next-door neighbors were here, but they didn't stay long. They're pretty good friends, especially Ellen," Mrs. Collins said with a wide smile. "I always call her Ellen, but I call her husband Mister Barlow. It seems more proper, you know, him being a man and all. Now their son, Andrew, he's a good boy, maybe a bit strange at times, but most boys his age are. He's 'bout seven years old." A finder under her cheek and a nibble on her tongue, she said, "No, he's not seven; he's eight years old. I remember 'cause I brought him into the world. That was eight years ago."

"So they left after you found your *Melissa* in the bathtub?" Officer Williams asked.

"Ain't you listening to me, Mister Williams?"

Williams corrected her again. "It's Officer Williams, ma'am, and I am listening to you. But someone had to come into the house to do what they did to your. . . your *Melissa*."

"I just told you, *Officer Williams*! Nobody was here but my neighbors, and they didn't stay long."

"Neighbors?" Officer Marten said.

"Yes, I told you my neighbors were here, the Barlows, Ellen and Mister Barlow and their boy, Andrew."

"Andy?" Williams asked.

"No! It's Andrew. He don't like being called A*ndy*, but I think Andy is a good name. But like I said, he don't like it, but he does like playing with my Melissa. Sometimes I'd see him outside petting her. He liked my Melissa, and she liked him. But today, he was playing with her right here on this couch, then she jumped out of his lap and ran into the kitchen. That's where she eats most of the time. He went to find her, I told him to do that, and he did, but he couldn't find her.

"They left a bit after that; the Barlows did, but they are good neighbors, but-" Tears began to run down her cheeks. "I don't know what I'll do without my Melissa. I remember I let her out one time, and she was gone for a whole day. I cried and asked God to bring her back, and he did. She came back meowing to get in at the back door, so I-"

Officer Marten interrupted with her in a comforting tone. "So you do you have a back door, Mrs. Collins?"

"I said I had one. A back door on the other side of the kitchen."

"Do you keep it locked?" Officer Williams asked.

"Why yes! Of course, I do, at least most of the time. But sometimes I open it to let my Melissa go out, so maybe it wasn't locked." Then she frowned. "I bet it was that man in that brown house next door. He's a Mexican, I think. You can't miss him. He's skinny, with wiry, black hair, and he has tattoos, a lot of tattoos; praying hands on one arm, and an angel on the other. I think the angel was on his right arm. Oh yes, he has one of those goatee beards, you know, just on the chin. That's stupid. If you want a beard, get a real beard. I bet it was him- it had to be him. He hates pets. I know he didn't like my Melissa. Once I caught him pushing her out of his way with his broom. That's who it's gotta be. You be careful; he might hurt you too."

After a brief silence, the officers looked at each other while Mrs. Collins wiped tears from her eyes. "Yes! I know it had to be him."

Officer Williams forced back a laugh. "Mrs. Collins, just think about it for a minute. Just because he doesn't like cats doesn't mean he hated them enough to sneak up the steps, open your back door, grab your cat, I mean your *Melissa*, and then drown her in the bathtub. Maybe you already had water in the tub and, your Melissa fell in and couldn't get out."

"I did have a bath this morning, but-"

"That's probably what happened, Mrs. Collins," Officer Williams said. "Your *Melissa* ran in the bathroom and-"

Officer Marten's glare cut her partner off. "Officer Williams is right, Mrs. Collins. It could have been an accident."

"No! It had to be him!" Mrs. Collins insisted. "It had to be."

"Mrs. Collins, we need proof that someone broke into your house, and we don't have any," Officer Marten said. Looking at her partner again, she continued. "But what we can do is help you bury your Melissa in the backyard."

"If that's the most you can do, I guess I appreciate you doing that. I think I have a shovel in the basement."

After putting Elissa to rest in the small grave they dug in the backyard, the Officers left shaking their heads while Mrs. Olivia Collins went back into the house. Without Melissa, she was now alone. "My poor Melissa," she mumbled. "Who could have done such a thing?"

43

CHAPTER V

Life was difficult for Mrs. Collins after losing her Melissa. A year of interrupted sleep and a year of mourning in the daytime took its effect on her mental and physical health. She began going house to house, asking neighbors if they had seen her cat. For the third time in the week, she knocked on David Ricardo's door.

David Ricardo was born in Mexico, but his parents migrated to Georgia when he was just a baby. He lived most of his life on Shadow Lane and was known to be a gentleman. If you needed a yard mowed or a porch cleaned, you could always depend on him. Although he was married, few people knew his younger wife. She was shy and spent most of her time in the house. Four years after their only child was born, she died in an auto accident. Although the accident was not his fault, he was driving. Guilt soon added to his deteriorating life. When the forty-year man looked into the mirror, he saw what his neighbors saw, a thin, ill-tempered man with facial wrinkles. Most people avoided him. Olivia Collins was not most people.

Mister Ricardo ignored the knock on his door. The shout that followed was more difficult to ignore. He returned the shout with one of his own. "Go away, old lady. I don't know where your damn cat is."

"Not a cat. It's Melissa. I know you know where she is. I'll call the police to come and investigate you?"

"You can call the police, but they won't come. They know you're crazy, so just leave me alone."

"I know you killed my Melissa. You won't get away with it," Mrs. Collins shouted as she started to leave. Then she stopped. "Mister Ricardo, this is Mrs. Collins next door. We haven't seen you much anymore. How are your wife and your little boy?"

"You crazy woman. You just accused me of killing your damn cat a minute ago, and now you want to know how my dead wife and my son are doing. They need to put you to an asylum."

"Seems you're busy. Maybe I can come back later. Now, if you see my Melissa, let me know. I live next door." Then she walked toward the Barlows house, calling, "Melissa, Melissa.

"Here comes that crazy lady next door again," Andrew said when he saw her coming across the yard.

"Andrew, she's not crazy. She just gets confused sometimes." Ellen said. "Besides, we seem to be the only friends the poor lady has anymore. If she comes here, you just tell her you haven't seen Melissa, but you'll keep your eye out for her."

"It's okay, Mom. She turned around. It looks like she's going back to her house."

"Andrew, you go over there and make sure she's okay."

"Mom, she ain't okay. She's crazy."

"She just gets confused sometimes, Andrew. A lot of old people have that problem, so just be patient with her. When you get old, it might happen to you," Ellen said as she swapped across his head. "I haven't seen much of her this week, so when you go trick or treating. Stop and check on her. Besides, she always likes to see how you dress up for on Halloween."

"Maybe my zombie costume will scare her."

Ellen laughed as she put the last of her makeup on Andrew's face. "You do look scary, but I think she can handle a zombie asking for treats, okay. Anyway, please check on her." Andrew sighed as he jotted to the house next door.

"Oh, my goodness!" Mrs. Collins said as she opened the door. "It's a zombie!"

"Boo!" Andrew said, then he laughed. "It's just me, Andrew, Mrs. Collins."

Mrs. Collins took a deep breath. "Why hello, Andrew. You had me scared for a minute. I bet you came to tell me you found my Melissa.

"No, ma'am. I ain't seen her since, well, a long time. It's Halloween, and I'm here trick or treating."

"I got some treats for a zombie. How about some cookies, the chocolate ones you like? Come on in and visit for a while. No one seems to come around anymore. I just don't know why."

"Just for a minute, Mrs. Collins, then I have to go and scare other people."

Mrs. Collins gave him a hand full of chocolate cookies and patted him on his ragged head covering. "Why you're outside, keep your eye out for my Melissa. She's the only family I got except for my daughter, and I don' see her much anymore, but-" Then, with eyes wide open and a smile, she said, "Wait, I think I hear my daughter. I bet she found my Melissa," she said as she wobbled to the back door."Now you just wait here while I let her in. She'll be glad to see you."

Several minutes later, Mrs. Collins came back to the living room. "It wasn't her, but she will-" Andrew was no longer there. "I bet he went out to look for my Melissa. Yes, I think he did. He's such a good boy." Then she heard a noise upstairs. "I bet Melissa is hiding up there."

An hour later, Andrew came home with a plastic pumpkin full of treats. "What did Mrs. Collins give you, Zombie boy?" Ellen asked as she washed the zombie pale white from his face.

"She gave me some cookies, and she wanted me to look for her cat again."

"She asks everyone to do that, but did she seem okay?"

"She was scared for a minute, but when I told her who I was, she was okay."

*   *   *

Mrs. Collins had a daily routine; a breakfast consisting of coffee and toast and an hour on the phone gossiping with the few neighbors who would answer her call. After that, rain or shine, she was on the porch in her rocking chair, waiting for the mailman. After two days of putting her mail into the mailbox instead of into her hand, the mailman became worried. His concern sent him knocking on her door. After several knocks, he turned the door knob. The door opened. "Mrs. Collins," he shouted, "This is Mister Jenkins, your mailman. I have some mail for you." There was no answer. Not sure what to do, he called her again. Still no answer. Two steps into the living room, he saw why there was no answer.

They buried Mrs. Collins in the cemetery behind the house she lived in most of her life. Only Pastor Garland, Mister Swartz, and the Barlows attended her funeral.

"Did she die because her cat died last year?" Andrew asked after the funeral.

Ellen pulled Andrew next to her on the couch. "Why would you think that?" she asked. "The police said it was an accident."

"Someone told me it was my fault for not finding her cat for her."

"That's ridiculous, Andrew. Did that Ricardo boy tell you that?"

"No. I don't play with him anymore. He's weird. He wanted me to sneak into Mrs. Collins' cellar and see what she hides down there. I told him no! He said he would hurt me I ever told anyone."

Ellen shook her head. "Mrs. Collins was right about that boy."

Suddenly Andrew's tone changed as he glared at his mother and then pulled away from her.

"I hate him. I wish he was dead too!"

"Andrew, that's a horrible thing for you to say. I don't want you to hate him or anybody else. Just stay away from him."

"What's all the noise in here?" Michael asked as he came into the room.

"Nothing, but your son being a weirdo."

"And I hate Mister Long Nose too!" Andrew shouted.

Ellen stopped what she was doing. "Why are you saying these things, Andrew? Mister Pinocchio's just a toy."

"He does bad things, and he blames me," Andrew shouted, then he pointed to his father. "And he doesn't like you either."

Ellen grabbed her son's arm and pulled him back to the couch. "Don't be silly, Andrew, and don't yell at your father like that."

Andrew glared at his father. "He's not my dad. My dad ran away. I think he's dead."

In shock, Michael looked at Ellen. "What in the hell is he talking about?"

Ellen tried to explain the unexplainable. "Don't pay him any mind, honey. It's just a little boy's imagination. He has these spells sometimes, but he gets over them."

Michael shook his head in frustration. "I hope so."

"Mommy, where's Mister Long Nose?"

"You mean the toy you just said you hated?" Ellen asked in surprise. "It's over there behind the chair where you left it."

"I love my Mister Long Nose. He's my favorite thing," Andrew said as he picked up Pinocchio. "I want to take him on a ride in my truck."

Trying to forget Andrew's impulsive behavior, Ellen gently swapped him on the head. "You and Mister Long Nose will have to wait until Mister Dad fixes your truck . . . like he said he would."

"Who broke it, Mommy?"

"Enough of the, *I don't know* stuff, Andrew. Just play with Mister Long Nose for now."

CHAPTER VI

It was the last day of the school week. With the weekend coming along with his birthday and Halloween, Andrew should have been eager to get the day started. However, Ellen had trouble getting him out of bed and even more trouble getting him dressed.

"But Mommy, I don't want to go to school," Andrew shouted as he tried to pull away from her grip on his hand.

"We've been over this all week. There will be no trick or treating tomorrow if you don't get up. Besides, you will be ten years old tomorrow, and school is for big boys and girls. I thought you were a big boy."

"Nobody likes me at school. Someone might hurt me like Billy did."

"Mister Ricardo's boy? I told you not to play with him."

"I don't anymore, Mom. He's mean. He wanted me to help him roll down that big rock on the outback into the road. I didn't, and he got mad. He might still be mad at me."

"Just stay away from him."

"But what if-"

"No *ifs*. Billy is a grade ahead of you, so you're not likely to run into him at school. If you do, just ignore him, and if he does bother you, tell your teacher."

"But Billy rides the bus too."

"The bus driver won't let him get out of hand, and the bus stops a block from our house. Now you behave, you hear me."

"But what about Billy?"

"Billy is a bully, Andrew, and bullies only pick on people who are afraid to stand up to them," Ellen said as she handed Andrew his lunch. "The best way to deal with a bully is to ignore him."

"What if that don't stop him?"

"Then you stand up to him." Ellen saw the fear in her son's face. "Don't worry now; I'll wait here for you to get on the bus, and I'll be out here when you come home."

"No! The other kids will just laugh at me. I'll be okay. If Billy bothers me, I'll just ignore him. If that doesn't work, I'll stand up to him like you said." That Friday morning, he had his chance.

Once in school, Andrew knew he would be safe. He also knew why Billy made him his target every chance he got. Billy was jealous of Andrew because his teacher, Mrs. Harris, had taken a liking to him because he always did his homework, and he was the first to raise his hand when she posted a question on the chalkboard. Add to that, Andrew was rewarded by being able to stay a few minutes to clean up tables after lunch, something given only to students who teachers thought were most responsible, something Billy had never earned.

When Andrew reached the bus stop, Billy teased one of

the girls. When he saw Andrew glaring at him, he started toward him, but the bus arrived before he could reach him. Laughing, he said, "Saved by the bus, Baby Barlow, but you gotta come home on it. See you then."

Andrew sat as close to the driver as he could. When the bus stopped, he ran to his classroom where he would be safe. Although he was able to avoid him during school hours, Billy was able to irritate him on the bus by plucking him on the back of the head if he could get a seat behind him or tripping him when he was getting on or off the bus. Andrew tried to ignore this.

While Andrew was waiting for the bus with other kids, Billy shoved him into the back of the girl he had been teasing that morning. When Andrew saw the bleeding cut on the girl's knee, he helped her up. "You need to get a band-aid on that cut," he said.

The girl was crying as she asked, "Why did he do that?"

"It's just because he's a bully."

"What makes him so mean?"

"My Mom said he's just jealous," Andrew said as he glared at Billy. When Billy responded vulgarly and stepped towards him, the girl and the other kids backed away and headed to their homes, leaving the two boys alone.

"Mommy! Mommy!"Billy shouted as he bumped his chest against Andrew. "Baby boy wants his mommy!"

"I don't need my mother to stand up to you because you're just a big-mouth bully who picks on girls."

Billy spat on Andrew's foot and pointed to the Barlow's home. "I guess you have to be brave living in that ugly house. My dad told me it's haunted, and anyone who lived there has to be weird. You live there, so that means you're weird."

Billy expected Andrew to back off or run to his house just a few yards away, but he didn't. Instead, he pushed Billy backward. "Don't say that about our house!"

Andrew's response surprised Billy. No one had ever stood up to him before. Trying to hide his astonishment, he waved his fist inches from Andrew's face. "And what are you going do about it?"

Andrew's blue eyes turned to deep green then his face began to change. It wasn't a change of anger or fear but a change that had no name. He pushed Billy's fisted hand away. "Let's go up to the graveyard, and I'll show you."

Billy had gone too far to back away. Hoping he would eventually back off, Billy pushed him again. "And who's gonna help you? Your dead brother up there!"

"Go up there with me, and you'll find out."

"Okay! Let's go, mommy's boy!"

"Not today. I have to get home, but how about tomorrow. Then we'll see how brave you are on Halloween in the graveyard."

*   *   *

Saturday morning Billy Ricardo left home to play. Eight hours later, he had not come back home. Mister Ricardo called the police. "This is Billy Ricardo's father," Mister Ricardo said over the phone. "My son went out to play this morning. He's been gone all day, but he hasn't come home yet."

"I wouldn't worry, Mister Ricardo," the officer said. "That's typical of young kids, especially boys."

"Not my boy, especially when he knew we were going to buy a Halloween costume for him. Besides, I've talked to all the boys who know him. One of the boys told me he saw him going to the cemetery to meet someone. After that, he never saw him again."

"Who was the other boy?"

"He didn't say."

"I'll pass this along to one of our officers, Mister Ricardo, but don't be surprised if your son pops up any time now."

On Saturday, Officer Marten and her partner talked to several of the kids in the neighborhood. Susan Johnson remembered the Billy–Andrew stand-off after getting off the school bus.

"Yesterday, Billy pushed me down," Susan mumbled, "and Andrew came to help me. They were really mad, at least Billy was, but he's always mad and picking a fight."

"Did they get into a fight?" Officer Marten asked.

"No, not then, but Billy told Andrew if he wanted to fight, he would meet him in the graveyard."

"What did Andrew say?"

"He said, *no*. At least, I heard him say that. He's not the type to get into arguments, and he's not the fighting kind, so he went on home. This morning, I saw Billy going up the hill towards the graveyard."

"Was he with anyone," Officer Williams asked.

"He was by himself when I saw him start up there, but I think he was just showing off. He talks a lot, but I would be surprised if he would go up there alone, especially on Halloween. He always said it was too spooky."

"Thanks, Susan," Officer Marten said as she shook the girl's hand. "You've been a lot of help."

As they walked away, Marten looked at her partner. "We better look up there anyway."

The officers searched the graveyard. Billy Ricardo was still there.

*   *   *

"Mrs. Barlow, we need to talk to your son," Officer Marten said when Ellen came to the door.

"Andrew? Has he done something wrong?"

"No, I don't think so.' After a minute of hesitation, Ellen nodded. "Andrew's in the living room playing with his toys. I'll get him for you, but I would like to know why you want to see him."

"One of the boys in the neighborhood was found dead in the graveyard, Mrs. Barlow," Officer Marten whispered.

"Oh, my God!" Ellen muttered as she put her hand over her mouth. "Who was it?"

"It was the Ricardo boy up the street.

We're talking to all of the kids in the neighborhood." Seeing the confusion on Ellen's face, Marten changed her tone. "Since the Ricardo boy was your son's friend, we wanted to know if he might have been with him earlier this afternoon."

"Friends? Andrew knows him, but they weren't friends. My son stayed away from him because-"

"Like Officer Marten said, Mrs. Barlow, this is just a routine investigation," Officer Williams explained. "We're talking to all the kids in the neighborhood. Andrew is the next on our list. Can we talk to him? It won't take long."

"You can talk to him, but I don't know what he can tell you."

Andrew was shooting his Nerf gun when the officers came into the living room. "Andrew, these police officers need to talk to you," Ellen said as she motioned for the officers to sit down.

"Happy birthday, Andrew," Marten said. "We won't take long, but I want to ask you a few questions. You know Billy Ricardo, don't you?"

Andrew nodded.

"And you're friends?"

Andrew shook his head. "I don't play with him; He's a bully."

"So you didn't play with him today? You didn't go up to the cemetery, the graveyard with him?"

"I didn't see him since yesterday when he wanted me to

57

go up to the graveyard and fight, but I didn't go. I knew he didn't want to play, he just wanted to fight, but I don't fight. I just came on to my house."

After talking to the officers, Ellen walked them to the door. "You don't think someone killed him, do you?"

Officer Marten looked at her partner, then back at Ellen. "No, ma'am, but it's a bit strange. Anyway, for now, we have to call it an accident since it looks like he was playing around the tombstones and slipped on one hitting his head.

"Hit his head on a tombstone?"

"Yes, ma'am. On the Jimm Barlow gravestone," Marten's partner said. "One of your family?"

"Yes, I have a son buried there."

"Sorry to hear that, ma'am," the officer said. "Although it seems to be an accident . . . a horrible accident, we still have to investigate it."

Although Billy's death shocked the Shadow Lane neighborhood, only the Barlows and two other families showed up at his funeral. To some, his death was just a shake of the head and a *SORRY FOR YOUR LOSS* card. Those who sent their children to public schools remembered only the trouble the dead boy brought to them and their children.

They buried Billy R. Ricardo on the other side of the cemetery from Jimm Barlow II.

CHAPTER VII

Sunday started as all Sundays on Shadow Lane started; early breakfast, quick showers, dressing, then off to church. As the Barlow's went past the Ricardo house, Ellen whispered to Michael, "The poor man is still mourning the loss of his son. He won't even go to church anymore."

"Oh, he'll be out later. He spends every Sunday in the graveyard talking to his son," Michael said. "We'll see him when we go to the cemetery."

"Why do we have to do that every Halloween, Mom?" Andrew asked.

"It's our way of telling Jimm we love him and miss him."

"Jimm?

"Yes, Andrew, your brother Jimm."

"Why does it make you cry when we go up there?"

"It's complicated and hard to explain, son," Michael said. "But this day in October is partly sad because of Jimm and partly happy because it's your birthday."

"You always tell me that my brother's up there. I don't know how I could have a brother if I was your only child. It don't make sense, Mom."

"You'll understand when you get older," Ellen said as she dropped down on one knee and put her arms around

Andrew. "For now, just accept that it's something important to your dad and me."

Andrew shrugged his shoulders then asked, "When can we have my birthday party?"

"After church and before you go trick or treating."

"Did you ask any of the other kids to come over?"

"I asked some to come, but their parents said they already have plans. So we'll have to celebrate alone."

After Pastor Garland greeted each one as they entered the small church, he started his ceremony as usual. "Lord, bless those who come to worship you. Touch the hearts of those who do not." Then he scanned the half-empty seats. "And send them a message that Hell awaits them if they don't change their ways, and those who sell their souls to Satan."

Ellen took a deep breath and squeezed Michael's hand as she remembered the words from the preacher when she needed him the most-*This thing was not born alive, so it doesn't have a soul, and it doesn't belong to God.*

Church ended with another warning from Pastor Garland. "Remember, this day is the devil's day. It is blasphemy to celebrate it by dressing up in costumes and begging people for treats, and if they don't, they threaten them with tricks. Remember, God sees you! So stay home and pray for those who side with the devil."

Ellen decided she would stay home rather than go back to his church.

As they did every October 31st, after leaving the church,

they headed to the cemetery with flowers for Jimm's grave. As they passed Mister Ricardo's house, Ellen saw the aging man looking out of the window. "I know what pain that poor man is going through," she whispered to Michael. "He needs that preacher's support, not his damnation."

Andrew ran ahead of them then stopped at the corner of the path leading up to the cemetery. Suddenly, the wind began blowing while dark clouds gathered. When Ellen and Michael caught up, Andrew pointed to the clouds. "Do we have to go up there if it rains?"

"If it rains, we have those things we call umbrellas," Michael said with a smile.

As the clouds gathered, they began to thin then gathered again over the cemetery. "That's a sudden change in the weather," Ellen said as she looked at the clouds that were now dark enough to carry a flood of rain. "You and Andrew go on up to the cemetery. I'll grab the flowers and the umbrellas and meet you there."

"I can still go trick or treating, can't I?"

Michael took Andrew's hand. "We'll have to see, but I think the clouds are just playing games with us." By the time they reached Jimm's grave, black clouds completely overshadowed the cemetery.

A few minutes later, Ellen showed up. Mister Ricardo was a few yards behind her. "I tried to talk to give him an umbrella," she said as she handed Michael one. "But he just shook his head and went to his son's grave."

After a few minutes of silent prayer, the sun broke through the clouds. Ellen reached for Andrew's hand. He was not there. "Where are . . ." Before she could finish her question, Andrew came running to them.

"I tried to tell Mister Ricardo I wished Billy could be here to go trick or treating with me, but he just gave me a scary look and walked away."

"Andrew, it's only been a year since the poor man lost his son. He's still mourning, so don't bother him," Ellen said as they left the graveyard.

After an early dinner, opening presents, and cake cutting, Andrew grabbed his Halloween costume. This year he was dressed as a fireman. Ellen helped him with his costume, then warned him not to stay out very long and for him not to bother Mister Ricardo.

When Andrew was ready to leave, she noticed he had the boy-scout knife he got for his birthday in his hand. "Andrew, that knife your dad gave you for your birthday is not a toy. Don't take it with you."

"Can I go to Mister Ricardo's house and show it to him?"

"No, Andrew. Just leave the man alone."

"Can't I just tell him I'm sorry a Billy?"

Ellen sighed deeply. "Okay. But make it short, and don't expect a treat," she said as she straightened out the hose over his shoulder. And don't try to play any trick on the old man!"

The small hose now wrapped around his shoulder,

traditional fireman hat on his head, plastic pumpkin in hand, Andrew knocked on Ricardo's door.

"Just go away!" Ricardo shouted.

"Mister Ricardo, it's just me, Andrew from next door."

"There's no treats here, boy. Just go away."

"But all I want to do is-"

Ricardo opened the door with a half-finished pint of alcohol in one hand and a 38 caliber revolver in the other. "I told you to go away, boy!"

"I just wanted to."

"This isn't a good time for anyone to come to my house," Ricardo said as he took a deep drink of whiskey from the pint he had leaned on all day. "Especially you, boy."

"I'm sorry, Mister Ricardo, but since I never told you I was sorry about Billy's accident, I thought I could do it now."

"It wasn't no accident, boy. You went up there with him; then they found him dead! It wasn't an accident, and you know it."

"No, sir. I went home. I don't know what happened, but-"

Ricardo took another drink of the cheap whiskey then started to shut the door. Andrew stepped inside before the door closed. Once inside, he glared at the intoxicated man. "Does drinking like that help you?"

"Just go on down the street, boy," Ricardo said as he took the last drink of whiskey then set the empty bottle down on the table next to Andrew.

"Mister Ricardo, I just wanted to say I was-" Andrew's

eyes widened as Ricardo waved the revolver at him. Andrew's eyes turned green. Abroad grin followed as he looked at the gun then up at the staggering man.

Andrew Barlow faded as *HE* appeared.

What you gonna do, shoot a little boy? Billy hated you. He told people about the bad things you did to him and his mother. Maybe that's why he died.

Mister Ricardo laid his gun on the table next to the bottle of whiskey and began crying. "I never hurt him or his mother. After she died from cancer, all I had left was Billy. I just want to know what happened up there!"

All you need to know about Billy is he's dead, Dead, and it's all your fault. Maybe you want to go and see him. You got a gun. You're just sitting there looking at it in your hand.

Then the boy laughed.

Why not use it, or do you need some help?

Shaking his head, Ricardo shouted, "Who are you? What are you?"

"Golly, Mister Ricardo, I just came by to make you feel better, but if-" Then Andrew's eyes focused at the revolver.

"Be careful with this. My dad said guns are dangerous." Then his voice changed as he picked up the gun and continued staring at it.

Better be careful, old man. You could hurt yourself with it.

"Put my gun down and get the hell out of here, boy, before I hurt you."

As Andrew ran back to his house, he saw his mother waiting on the porch. "Andrew, are you okay? What was that a loud bang I heard?"

"I don't know, Mom. It sounded like a firecracker," Andrew said as he swung his empty plastic pumpkin. "Can I go trick or treating now?"

"Okay, Mister, eleven-year-old boy. But be careful and don't stay out long."

After hugging his mother, Andrew ran past Mister Ricardo's house and met up with the other kids living on Shadow Lane.

* * *

Officer Marten was just checking out of the police station when the call came in. "Hold on there, Jessica," the duty officer said. "I just got a call from someone on Shadow Lane saying he heard a gunshot. Your area, isn't it?"

Marten took a deep breath and sighed. "Yes, George, it's

my area, but can't you pass it on to someone else since I'm on my way home?" Home for Marten was a two-bedroom apartment, a fading television, a soft bed, a freezer full of *ready-to-cook* meals, and a promise that if she was ever advanced in her job, finding a house of her own was the first thing she would do.

Marten stopped then turned around. "Odds are it's going to be just another *gunshot* that's going to turn out to be a car backfiring," she muttered. "Who called?"

"A Mister Barlow."

"Michael Barlow? Yea, George, I know him."

"So you're going to handle it?"

Marten inhaled and nodded.

"I'll call your partner."

"No need to bother him," Marten grumbled. "He's halfway home by now."

"It's policy, Jessica. Never go on the street alone."

Marten shook her head. "Come on, George. I can handle this alone."

Knowing Marten would do what she wanted to do, George shrugged his shoulders. "Like you said, Jess, it's probably just a firecracker or some broken down car backfiring."

* * *

"Good to see you again, Mister Barlow," Detective

Marten said as she shook Michael's hand. "You called the station about hearing a gunshot?"

"I wasn't here," Michael stammered, "but my son and my wife were. My son, Andrew, said it might not be anything other than a firecracker or a car backfiring, but not many cars come this far up the Lane. My wife said it sounded more like a gunshot, but she wasn't sure, so I thought the best thing to do was to let the police know about it. With it being Halloween, I guess it could have been anything."

"Well, let's hope that was all it was. Any idea where it came from?"

"I was in the house when I heard the noise," Ellen said, "but I wasn't clear where it came from."

"Did anyone else hear it?" Marten asked.

"Our son, Andrew, was playing outside, and he heard it. He thought it was a firecracker," Ellen said, "but I thought it sounded too loud for that."

Andrew stepped forward. "Yes, ma'am, I was outside when I heard it. I was going trick or treating, then there was a big bang, like a big firecracker."

"Was there anyone outside with you?" Marten asked.

Andrew just shrugged his shoulders. "Maybe, but I didn't see anybody." After a minute of thought, he pointed to Ricardo's house, two houses away. "It sounded close to his house. Maybe he knows what it was." Then he turned to his father. "Dad, can I go and ask him?"

Officer Marten shook her head. "Thanks, but that's my

job. You just go on in the house and start working on that pumpkin full of goodies." She watched as Andrew went into the house then nodded to Michael. "A pretty good kid you got there, Mister Barlow. It could have been a firecracker or a car backfiring. Both can be pretty loud. Anyway, I'll ask a few of the people living around here if they heard anything."

Michael and Ellen went into the house while Officer Marten started knocking on doors. She began with the Ricardo house. She didn't have to go any further.

CHAPTER VIII

It had been almost a year since Mister Ricardo's suicide when Randy Jackson and his wife, Maya, bought Mrs. Collin's house. During his third tour in Afghanistan, a land mine wounded him physically and emotionally. After a year of treatment in the Navy hospital, the Marine Corps discharged him with one-hundred percent disability.

Brown-skinned, five-foot, one-hundred-pound Maya had been his nurse during his hospitalization as well after his discharge. Emotionally suffering from Posttraumatic Stress Disorder and sensitivity about his facial scars, Randy was more withdrawn. Add to that, his living in Savannah, where his race was all too often sneered.

Michael was now in a manager position for NationWide Freight. Randy needed a job; Nation Wide Freight needed drivers. Wide Freight was quick to hire him.   Despite both Randy and Maya being in their mid-twenties, Michael and Ellen became close friends with their new neighbors. Not having children of her own, Maya took an interest in Andrew, who she called *Andy*.

When Maya met Ellen for their daily morning coffee, Andrew had already left on the school bus.

"You seem to be in a bad mood this morning, Ellen. Anything wrong?"

After a deep sigh, Ellen said, "Just that boy of mine.

I'm tired of asking him, *who did this, who did that, who broke the lamp, who broke the porch swing! Now,* it's, *who broke my favorite dishes,*" she muttered as she picked up the last of what she called the *dining room plates* from the floor. "All I ever get from Andrew is, *I don't know, Mom!'*

After tossing the glass into the garbage can, Ellen poured two cups of coffee. "Not to mention all the times he was either held after school or sent home early because of his behavior. He just finished a two-day suspension for a classroom event with his teacher."

"Come on, Ellen, even good boys have episodes at his age, and Andy is a good boy."

"I know, despite all of that," Ellen said. "He still gets great grades when he is in school. And most of the time he can be as sweet as your sweet potato pie, then, bingo-"

"Randy and I want to have children, but it doesn't seem like it's going to happen. So I just appreciate him."

"I know how that is. I complain a lot, but I couldn't get along without him," Ellen said as she refilled their coffee cups.

"What happened to the other boy," Maya asked as she sipped on her coffee.

"I don't like to talk about that."

"I'm sorry," Maya mumbled. "Maybe I shouldn't have asked, but when we went exploring at the cemetery yesterday, we saw a gravestone for Olivia Collins between Henry

Collins and Rachel Collins," Maya continued with a grin. I figured they were the folks that-" she snickered and shook her head. *Folks? Just listen to me. I'm turning into a real Georgian.* Anyway, we figured it was the family who owned the house we bought. Then we saw a gravestone with a boy named Jimm Barlow II on it. We assumed it was one of your children."

"It's was," Ellen moaned. "Jimm and Andrew were twins or should have been-" Ellen lowered her head and dabbed at a teardrop on her cheek. "I'm sorry, but I just have difficulty talking about it."

"Anyway, I'm sorry I brought it up. Hasn't Andy ever asked you about him?"

"Asked about him? No, but I've often wondered why he hasn't. At the same time, I'm glad he hasn't. It's like I said, it's difficult for an adult to understand, much less a child."

"I might understand. Try me."

There were minutes of quietness as Ellen's mind went back eleven years. *Flattened, paper-thin, parchment-like, fetus remnant, vanishing twin. It should have been a baby, a twin baby.* "I haven't discussed this with anyone since Mrs. Collins was here. She was a bit weird, but she was a good midwife and a good friend. She delivered Andrew and what happened was something rare; rare and shocking."

After hearing her story, Ellen looked at Maya's furrowed brow showing she was puzzled but not shocked. "So Andy doesn't know about this?"

"If most adults don't understand it, how could a boy?"

"He might not understand what happened to his brother," Maya said, "but he has to wonder about *having* a brother, a twin brother at that. And he knows his birthday, and he knows the birthday on the tombstone in the graveyard. He can do the math."

Ellen lowered her head and was quiet for a minute, then looked at Maya. "Michael thinks we should tell him too. Not everything, but something. If we do, just how much should we tell him?"

Maya dismissed the question with another narrowing of her brows. "Maybe it would be easier if you let a professional help you. You know, a child psychologist."

Ellen shook her head. "He's not crazy, Maya."

"I know he's not crazy, but a professional opinion won't hurt. Maybe we can talk about it again tomorrow," Maya said as she looked at her watch. "I have to run some errands and get Randy something for dinner."

Ellen spent the rest of the day listening to Maya's suggestion. Still, she couldn't decide what was best for Andrew or what was best for her. Before she realized it, it was past time to meet Andrew at the bus stop. The bus had left, leaving Andrew alone on the sidewalk. Although alone, when she approached him, he seemed to be talking to someone.

"Andrew, who are you talking to?"

"Just my friend, Mom."

"Your friend?" Ellen asked. "Andrew, no one is here but you and me."

"I know, Mom. He's gone now. He wanted me to go to the graveyard and play. I told him maybe later, but you would be here, and then you were."

Ellen shook her head. "You can be weird sometimes, Andrew Barlow."

Once home, she made him a snack to hold him until dinner. "Made your favorite, a banana, and peanut butter sandwich. Should I make one for your friend too?"

Andrew laughed and hugged Ellen. "Now, who's being weird, Mom?"

As she watched him eating, she asked herself, *how could he be so wonderful yet have these anger spells? Maybe Maya was right. He might need professional help.* For now, she decided to push the troubling thought away and deal with the present. "How was school today?" she asked.

"Pretty good. I got all A's on my math test."

Ellen smiled. "You're a smart boy, and I'm proud of you." Then she decided this would be as good as time as any to have them *don't know Mom* discussion. "There's something else we need to talk about."

Andrew did not respond.

"We need to talk about things you do at home and school. Things like misbehaving at school, breaking a toy here at home, and when I ask you why you did them, all you say is, *I don't know who did it.*"

"Mom, I don't lie. I don't know who does those things. All I know is I didn't do them."

"Andrew, you're almost twelve years old now. You've got to start taking responsibility, but if you don't remember doing these things, maybe we need to take you to a doctor and find out why."

No! No! Doctors are dangerous.

Not being sure where the voice came from, Andrew repeated it. "No! Doctors are dangerous."

"Don't be ridiculous. Doctors help people. Do you remember when you had to have your tonsils taken out and when you had measles? Those times you just ran a fever and couldn't go to school. Then there was the time you almost broke your leg."

"I know, Mom. I know. I didn't mean it about the doctors."

"Then why did you say they were dangerous?"

"I don't know. *He* told me to say that."

Ellen stopped what she was doing and put her hands on Andrew's shoulders. "Andrew Barlow! Who told you to say that? I'm the only one here with you, and I know I didn't say that."

Andrew put his face in cupped hands and began to cry.

Don't be a wimp, Brother!

Andrew threw his fork across the room and shouted, "I'm not a wimp, and I'm not your-"

Ellen's concern frustration turned to panic as she wrapped her arms around her son. "You're not what, Andrew?"

"Nothing, Mom."

Ellen's response was one of fear. "Andrew Barlow," you just shouted at me and threw a fork across the table, so don't say it's nothing!"

"I wasn't shouting at you, and I'm sorry about the fork."

"It's okay," Ellen said as she put her arms around Andrew. "Honey, just tell me what set you off like that."

Andrew laid his head on the table and started crying again. "I can't explain it, Mom. I just can't," he muttered as he pushed away from her mother.

Ellen wasn't sure if what she saw and heard were coming from confusion or if they were cries for help, which of the two didn't matter. They had to address both of them. "It's okay," Ellen said with an irritable tone. "Dad will be home soon. We can discuss this when he gets here."

*   *   *

Ellen had already cleaned up in the kitchen when Michael came home. Instead of meeting him with a, *Go clean up, dinners almost ready,* she was staring out the kitchen window.

Thinking she was mad because he was late and didn't call her, Michael put his hand on her shoulder. Ellen jerked away from the unexpected touch. "Honey, I'm sorry I didn't call you, but we had a truck involved in an accident. No one was hurt, but the paperwork; you know how that is."

Ellen jumped back and took a deep breath.

Michael looked at her still in her robe. "It's not like you to be so jumpy, honey. Are you okay?"

Ellen smiled. "It's okay. I didn't hear you come in, and you scared me, that's all."

"Sorry, honey."

"It's okay," Ellen said as she rubbed her hand through her messy hair. Not being dressed and her hair out of place was just as unusual as Michael coming home late. "I guess I'm just tired."

Her tone and indifference troubled him. "Are you sure nothing's wrong?" When Ellen didn't answer, he looked into the living room. "Where's Andrew?"

"He's next door. Maya got a new pet, and she wanted him to help her find a good name for it."

"Hope it's not a barking dog."

"No, just a parakeet," Ellen said as she tried to change her frown into a smile.

"A parakeet? You must be kidding!"

"Yes, dear," Ellen mocked. "I am kidding. He needs a dog, a small one, but a dog."

"Sorry! I'll keep my eye out for one."

Ellen tapped the back of his head. "NO! You will get one. There's plenty at the animal shelter downtown. Just make sure it's small and doesn't shed-I'm thinking a beagle."

"We can talk about dogs later," Michael muttered, "but now . . ."

"I know. Now you're hungry. Go clean up. It'll only take a few minutes to heat your dinner."

"Dinner can wait. But *something* is bothering you."

"You eat first; then we can talk."

Michael shook his head. "We talk while we eat!"

"Okay," Ellen said as she hugged him then heated his dinner. Once at the table, she took a deep breath. "Something is wrong with Andrew. Earlier today, I was talking to Maya. Then I talked to Mrs. Collins." Looking at Michael's raised brows, she laughed. "No, I haven't lost my mind.

"My talk with Mrs. Collins was usually a one-way conversation. Although I had to listen to her gossip for hours, she was a good listener at times, and she usually had good advice. There are times I wish she was still here. If she was, I think she would agree with Maya that our son needs help." Then she broke down and cried.

"It's good to talk to Maya. She seems to know a lot about psychology."

"Yes, she does," Ellen said as she wiped away her tears with the back of her hand. "I'll talk to her again tomorrow."

"It's early," Michael said. "Andrew will be playing with his toys until we make him go to bed. Why not now when we both are here?"

Just minutes after talking on the phone, Maya knocked on their door. "I'm not a doctor, Ellen," she said. "But from what you tell me, autism, ADHC, early psychological illness are all possibilities."

"Oh, my God," Ellen said muffled with her mouth under her hand.

"Ellen, I said they're *possible* . . . that doesn't mean they are likely," Maya said as she took Ellen's hand. "Still, I think he should see a doctor. Not the measles or chickenpox type, but a behavioral specialist who deals with children. I know one who deals with this type of behavior in children."

"I don't know, Maya."

"I think he's just what you need."

"Are you sure? I don't want some quack making things worse."

Maya smiled. "He's not a quack, Ellen. He's a behavioral specialist who deals with children like Andrew. Trust me; I used to wor

k for him."

*   *   *

Ellen was surprised to see Michael home so early in the middle of the week. "Oh, my God! she stammered. "What's wrong now?" She tossed her kitchen towel across the sink and ran to the door porch. "I see you've been shopping," she teased.

"Just doing what you told me to do."

"He's pretty. What kind is it?"

"Beagle! isn't it what you asked for?"

Ellen shot him a mocked frown.

Michael responded with, "Well, at least part Beagle."

"What is the-"

"Don't ask! I don't know what the other part is. Anyway, I think Andrew will like him."

When Ellen patted the dog's head, it growled. "It's okay, boy. No one's going to hurt you." The dog rewarded the soft tone and touch with a sloppy, wet tongue over her hand. "Where did you get him?" she asked as she wiped her hand across her kitchen apron.

"At the animal shelter. Do you think Andrew will like him?"

"Like him!" Ellen shouted. He'll be home soon. "He's going to love him."

"What's his name?"

"I don't think he has one, but he seems to growl a lot for no reason, so how about Growly?"

CHAPTER IX

ELLEN HEARD HIM STIRRING AROUND IN HIS ROOM WHEN Andrew should be asleep. Occasionally she would crack open his door to check on him. Sometimes he would be talking to Pinocchio or Growly; other times, he would just mutter to himself. When Ellen would ask him if anything was wrong, he always said, *I'm okay, Mommy, I'm just not tired yet.* This night was different.

"Why do you want to come with us, Mister Long Nose?" he muttered. After a pause, he nodded. "Okay, you can come, but it's our secret." As if in a trance, with Pinocchio in one hand, the banister rail in the other, and Growly just a step behind, he climbed the steps to the second floor. From the lone window, he watched as dark clouds floated over the sky, playing peek-a-boo with the rising full moon. Then *He* spoke.

> *Be careful! You're like a bird being pushed out*
> *of the nest by its mother. She wants to break*
> *us apart.*

Andrew tried to ignore the voice as the fading clouds gave way to the moon's fullness and brightness. While picking Pinocchio off the dust-ridden floor, he smiled and patted his dog's head. "Browser, Mister Long Nose said we have to go back downstairs cause it's bedtime."

*   *   *

Ellen was just getting out of the shower when sunlight hit their bedroom window. Michael was already on his second cup of coffee. "Maya's going to call someone who knows about children and mental stuff. She's going to see if he can see us today," she said as she grabbed the towel Michael tossed to her. "But it's not likely he'll be able to squeeze us in on such short notice."

"I can go with you if you want."

"There's no need for you to miss a day's work. Besides, we might go shopping."

"Andrew was up late last night again," Michael said as he finished his cup of coffee."

"I know. I could hear him talking to himself on the attic steps again. In case the doctor can see him. I'm going to keep him home just in case the doctor can see him today. But you go on to work. Maya and I can handle this."

It was early afternoon when Maya knocked on Ellen's door. "Good news," she beamed. "I called Doctor Ramirez this morning. He's the child psychologist I told you about. He had a cancellation. So he can see you and Andy today at one o'clock."

*   *   *

Doctor Ramirez's office was only twenty minutes away from the Barlow house. His dark skin and his speech showed he was of Indian orientation. "Mrs. Barlow, Maya told me a little about Andy."

"My name's not Andy," Andrew said with a sneer.

"I'm sorry, Andrew. How old are you, eleven? Twelve?"

Andrew nodded. "Eleven, but I'll be twelve in a few months."

"Mrs. Maya told me you're pretty smart for your age," Ramirez said as he motioned to his assistant. "This is Mrs. Simmons. She's going to take you into our playroom. There are plenty of things in there for a boy your age. I'll talk to you later, but I want to talk with your parents first."

"Why can't I go too?"

"It's about doctor stuff," Ramirez said. "Things you would find boring." Doctor Ramirez watched as Andrew left the room. "Seems like a typical pre-teen boy to me, but tell me, what concerns you enough to think he needs my help?"

Ellen sighed then closed her eyes briefly as she thought about what brought her the point of seeing a Psychologist. "I don't know where to start. I'm not even sure his behavior is abnormal, at least for a boy his age. Most of the time, he's pretty normal, but it's the times he's not normal that worries me."

"And what do you see as abnormal?"

"He goes from *Love you, Mom*, to sudden anger without any reason. Then later, he seems like he doesn't know he changed and denies his behavior," Ellen said as she took a deep breath. "Then there are times he blames things on some imaginary friend."

"I've seen this behavior change myself," Maya added. "At first, I thought it was like Ellen said, pre-teenage stuff, but now I'm not so sure."

"You both might be right, but it's apparent you are concerned about it, or you wouldn't be here. Anyway, we can use tests that might help find out what is wrong, if anything *is* wrong at all, Mrs. Barlow."

"No medicines?"

"No, no medicines," Ramirez said. "We deal more in *talk therapy* to make behavior changes. How we talk and what we talk about can be very useful for most children. While a few psychiatrists dangle in behavior disorders, most of them only deal with severe mental health conditions, conditions that would more likely respond to medicines.

"Now, I'm not dismissing psychiatrists, but there are a few that are too quick to prescribe medications, strong medications that have strong side effects when medicines aren't always needed," he said. "Psychologists, like me, can't prescribe medication, but that's okay. Talking and testing can do a lot for making a diagnosis."

"What tests?"

"There's a lot out there, but I usually start with the Rorschach. It's often called an *inkblot test* and the Wechsler Intelligence Scale test, but the Wechsler would be a waste of time since his intelligence is not in question. Other tests would depend on what comes out of our talks and the results of the Rorschach. We can start with you, Misses Barlow. Is there any family history of mental illness in your family?"

"Not that I know of, but I did have a period of depression, but I wouldn't call it a mental breakdown."

"Do you have children other than Andrew?"

"No, none living."

"Tell me about the one that died."

"Like I told Maya, it's complicated."

"I do *complicated* every day, Mrs. Barlow."

Ellen frowned. "That was a long time ago, Doctor. We dealt with it and moved on. I don't want to go into details now."

Andrew's first session with Doctor Ramirez was the following Friday. After Andrew's brief visit with Ramirez, his anger became worse. Broken toys, and school behavior, worsened to the extent the principal met with the Barlows, suggesting that *our school might not be the best place for Andrew.* Ellen decided she would teach him at home until they could afford to enroll him in a private school.

*   *   *

When Friday came, Michael insisted on going to the psychology appointment with her. "Do you want Maya to go too?" he asked.

"No, I think we've put her out enough. Besides, she

hasn't felt well these last few days. Something to do with her diabetes."

Andrew was eating his breakfast when he heard them talking. "I want Mrs. Maya to come with us," he said as he left the kitchen with a half-empty bowl of cereal.

"She can't, Andrew. I said she was not feeling well. You can see her when you get back."

"I want to see her now!" he responded as he threw his bowl against the wall sending milk and flakes across the room. "If she can't go, I'm not going."

"Andrew, I'm tired of this behavior," Michael said in an unusual stern voice. "That's why you're seeing a doctor. So clean up the mess you made and get ready to go."

"I'll get it," Ellen said. "And both of you calm down. My nerves will only take so much."

"Maya hates me. I know she hates me," Andrew said as he started to the upstairs attic.

"Where are you going?" Michael yelled. "Get your ass back down here."

"Dad, my friend doesn't like you yelling at me."

Michael regained his posture. "I don't care what your invisible friend likes-" Ellen's shaking head cut him off long enough for him to calm down. "I'm sorry about yelling, son," Michael grunted.

Ellen smiled and put her hand on Michael's hand. "What Dad means, Andrew is that Maya does like you; she likes you a lot, and you know it. It's just that she can't go today."

Andrew hesitated on the steps. "Is her diabetes going to kill her?" he asked as he turned around and came back down to the living room.

Ellen met him at the last step and put her arms around him. "No, no. She's not going to die. She takes shots to control her sugar. But she said she would go with us next time."

Andrew pulled away from his mother and ran to Michael. "I'm sorry, Dad. That wasn't me. It was-"

"I know it wasn't you, son. And I'm sorry I got mad."

As they headed towards the door, Andrew stopped and gazed up the stairs into the darkened hallway. "I get scared sometimes, Dad. Maybe we should move."

*   *   *

Doctor Ramirez was with another patient when Michaels and Ellen arrived for his arranged testing. "Someone will be with you in a few minutes," the woman at the sign-in desk said as she pointed to one of the empty seats.

Michael grabbed one of the year-old magazines and thumbed through the pages. "For what they charge," he muttered, "they should have something recent to read."

"We're not here to be entertained, honey," Ellen said. Seeing Andrew was worried, she put her arm around him. "There's nothing to be worried about; just some tests. I bet you'll pass every one of them."

When the door opened, a young woman entered the waiting room. "Mrs. Barlow, I'm Kelly, Doctor Ramirez's assistant," she said. "I'll be doing Andy's testing." Then she looked at Andrew. "No need to be scared, Andy?"

"My name's not Andy; it's Andrew!"

"Okay, Andrew, are you ready for the tests?"

"Andrew, remember, it's like Maya told you," Ellen interrupted. "It's like a school test, and you always do good on school tests."

"Your Mom's right, Andrew," Kelly said with a wide smile. "It's a lot like school tests, except you don't have to worry about failing. Just give the answer you think is right."

What seemed like hours to Ellen took only forty minutes.

"How did he do," she asked.

"He did just fine," Kelly said.

"What did it show," Michael asked.

"I'll have to go over them with Doctor Ramirez. That will take a few days, but he'll talk to this young man in a few minutes. You can leave him with us and come back in about an hour if you want, or you're welcome to wait here."

"We'll wait," Michael said as Kelly reached for Andrew's hand.

At first, Andrew pulled back, but Kelly just smiled. "There's nothing to be afraid about," she said. "All you and the doctor will do is talk. I think you'll find his office is a lot of fun."

Ramirez met Andrew at his office door. Once inside, Andrew felt relief. Disney characters decorated the walls with a Teddy bear sitting on a small chair. Ramirez's desk looked more like a child's table than a professional's desk.

"Andrew, it's like Miss Kelly said, we're going to talk, that's all," Doctor Ramirez said as he pointed to the stuffed chair next to his desk.

Andrew looked around the room with walls filled with Disney characters, a box of toys, and several puzzles on a side table.

"Why don't you have Pinocchio on the wall?"

"You're right. I should have a Pinocchio picture there. I'll look into it."

"I have a Mister Pinocchio at home," Andrew said. "He has a long nose because he tells lies sometimes."

I know all about Pinocchio, but I want to learn more about you, what you think about some things. What you like and don't like. And if there's something you don't want to talk to me about, you can talk to Mister Cuddly," Doctor Ramirez said as he pointed to the Teddy Bear. "He's good at keeping secrets, and he never lies, and there's another part of your visit that all of my patients like . . . you get to go to sleep for a while."

After twenty minutes of asking Andrew general things: *How's school? Do you sleep a lot or have dreams? How are your friends? Do you like to be left alone or prefer being with other people?* Finally, he came to the *sleep* part.

"Now, I want to see if I can put you to sleep for a few minutes."

"But I'm not tired."

"That's okay, Andrew. Just relax, and focus on this coin dangling from the chain. It will be just like having a daydream. Just clear your thoughts of everything other than the swinging coin. Take deep breaths and relax."

Andrew's breathing slowed as he closed his eyes.

"That's it, Andrew, focus . . . focus . . . focus on the swinging star."

Doctor Ramirez was good at hypnosis. It took only a few minutes before Andrew went into rapid eye movements and flickering, followed by slight jerks of his hands. Then he lowered his head and relaxed. Finally, he drifted away from his world into another.

"Just relax, now, Andrew. You're in a deep sleep, Andrew. All you can hear is my voice. Where are you now?" Ramirez whispered.

"*I don't know, but It's a quiet place, and it's warm. I'm all alone except for my shadow. I hear water running somewhere; maybe it's a river. The sun is getting hot now. My shadow doesn't like it; Make it go away.*"

"It's just your shadow, Andrew. It only does what you do, so ignore it. Focus on my words. Tell me about your life, things you like, and things that bother you."

"*No! Make the sun go away so my shadow will go too. He does bad things then blames me for them.*"

"It's okay now, Andrew. Clouds are beginning to block out the sun now. Your shadow is fading away."

"It's getting darker, but my shadow is still here. It's going one way, and I'm going another. Wait, I see a waterfall and a lot of people just looking at it. The waterfall sounds like it's angry."

"Ignore the waterfall, Andrew. Just tell me who the people are. Do you know them?"

"Mom and Dad are there with another woman. Mrs. Collins, I think. No, it's Mrs. Jackson. I like her a lot."

"Do they know you're there?"

"I don't think they know."

"Can you hear what they're talking about?"

"No, but my shadow can. It makes him mad. Maybe I'm just having a nightmare; I have a lot of them.."

"Get closer to her, Andrew, and see if you can hear what she's saying."

"Okay.". After muttering understandable words, Andrew continued. *"I can hear Mrs. Jackson better now, but I don't understand what she's saying, but she's makingMommy sad."*

"What do you think Mrs. Jackson is saying that makes her so sad?"

"It's something bad, something Mommy lost somewhere. I don't know what. Mrs. Jackson's whispering to Mommy now."

"Can you hear what she's saying?"

"It's something important."

Andrew shook his head and began muttering again.

Mommy's crying now, and she's really mad.

"Try hard to find out what's making her so mad, Andrew?"

"I'm trying, but they don't want me to hear them, so they're whispering."

"Try hard to hear them, Andrew. It's important to hear their secret."

"I can hear some of what she's saying now. It's about something the preacher said."

More shaking-More mumbling.

"Just relax, Andrew. Everything's going to be okay; just try to hear what the preacher said?"

"It's something bad, really bad. They don't want me to know about it, but He knows, and it makes Him mad."

"It's okay, Andrew. Tell me who *Him* is."

Andrew was whispering now. *"He won't let me."* "It's okay, we don't want to make *Him* mad, but can you tell me what Pastor Garland said?"

"He said, 'this thing doesn't have a soul."

"Doesn't have a soul! What does that mean?"

"I don't know what soul means.

Andrew's eyes began to flutter again. After a long pause, he continued.

"Someone else is coming here now."

"Who's coming, Andrew?"

"It's my shadow. It knows what the preacher said, but it won't tell me. It don't like Dad being there either".

"Why would your shadow make your dad mad?"

"*I don't know, but my shadow makes everybody mad. Even me sometimes. Stop!*"

"Stop what?"

"*He's shaking Mister Long Nose now.*"

"Why would he do that?"

"*Cause he knows it makes me mad. Dad's trying to take him away from him, but the shadow keeps pulling. He knows it's mine; he knows dad bought it for me.*"

Andrew's breathing is coming more rapid and deeper now.

Andrew began to shiver as his breathing became more rapid and deeper. "*Now he's throwing Mister Long Nose into the waterfall. Everybody's staring at me like it's my fault. I think they're mad at me too. I'm scared!*"

Doctor Ramirez realized that whatever Andrew was hearing and seeing was frightful, so he began to pull him back into the present.

After a half-hour in a deep sleep, Ramirez woke Andrew. "You had a good sleep, Andrew. How do you feel?"

"I had a dream. I think I did anyway."

"A dream? Tell me what you remember about it."

"I can't."

"You can't? Why can't you?"

"*He'll be mad!*"

"Who will get mad? Your dad?"

"No! *Him!*"

"Can you tell me who *Him* is?"

"He says he's my brother, but he's just my friend. He just wants to be part of our family, but they won't let him."

"But you're the only child, Andrew. Why would someone think you had a brother?"

Andrew whispered as he looked around the room, then up at the doctor, "Nobody, I guess. It must have been a dream."

Ramirez looked at Andrew then nodded. "Dreams can be scary things sometimes, can't they?" Then he walked Andrew back to the waiting room where Ellen and Michael were waiting.

"How did things go?" Ellen asked as she hugged Andrew.

"He was a good patient."

"So everything's okay?"

"I'm not sure, Mrs. Barlow. All I can tell you now is that his sleep session was a little troublesome."

"Troublesome? What does that mean?" Ellen asked as she began to cry. "Is there something . . ." Wanting not to worry Andrew, she stopped and looked at him then continued. "Is it something we should be worried about?"

Doctor Ramirez answered with a closed-mouth smile, then said, "Probably nothing, Mrs. Barlow. Andrew is likely to be a normal boy with exaggerated imagination. I see a lot of that, but I'll know more after reviewing the psychometric tests. That'll take a couple of days. After that, I'll have a better picture of what's going on, if anything. I'll have the desk set you up with another appointment."

Other than Andrew telling how he went to sleep and didn't even know it, the drive back to their house was quiet. When they arrived, Andrew went to his room and picked up Mister Long Nose. Then the voice came again:

Why did you tell him about me?

CHAPTER X

KELLY PUT ANDREW'S TEST RESULTS ON DOCTOR RAMIREZ'S desk, then shook her head. "Doctor, I scanned the Barlow boy's studies, but I can't get much out of them."

"He's an intelligent boy," Ramirez said as he thumbed through the six pages. "But some of the pictures he drew put him all over the scale when it comes to a diagnosis. Something is going on in his mind."

"The picture of his family I asked him to draw caught my eye might help," Kelly said as she pulled out one of the sheets of paper. "This is what he drew."

Ramirez looked at the pencil-drawn picture that showed a stick figure with names on each, *mother*, a *father*, *two boys*, one with his name over it, *brother* over the other. "I see what you mean," Ramirez said. "But why a second boy when he's the only child?"

"A good question," Kelly replied.

"What about the rest of the test?"

"His answers were all over the board," Kelly said as she handed Ramirez several studies.

Ramirez looked at the tests then shook his head. "If I had only one session with the boy to go on, I'd have to say he's normal for his age, but these studies show he's anything but normal."

"Maybe he's just playing us."

"Boys his age don't play games with psychometric tests. They design the tests to prevent that."

"Maybe he's hiding something?"

Ramirez took a deep breath. "The question is, what does he have to hide?"

"You're the psychologist, not me."

"Thanks, Kelly! That helps me a lot," Ramirez said as he put the file back on his desk. "Get the clerk to set up another appointment with the Barlows . . . but just with the parents."

*   *   *

Maya was having coffee with Ellen when the phone rang. After a minute of silence on her end, Ellen's face made it clear that the call was more than a friendly one.

"About Andrew?" Maya asked.

"Yes. It's Doctor Ramirez."

"Sound like things didn't go so good?"

"He made an appointment for Michael and me to see him tomorrow."

"Not with Andrew?" Maya asked.

"No. Just me and Michael. Other than that, he was vague, but I could tell by his tone bad news was coming." Elbows on the table, hands covering her face, Ellen sighed. "I hate to ask you, but can you watch Andrew tomorrow afternoon?"

"Ellen, I'm always here for you . . . and Andrew."

"I worry that maybe we went to the wrong doctor."

Maya moved her chair closer to Ellen. "Doctor Ramirez is one of the best. I've known him for years. We served together in Afghanistan. He was an army psychologist then, and I was just an army corporal. We came back to the states at the same time. He ended at Tuttle Army Health Clinic, where I was just a clerk. That was supposed to be a temporary job until I went to go to college to get a Nurses' degree, maybe even a doctorate, and become a psychologist."

"What stopped you?"

"Short story is, Randy. The long story is that Randy was serving his third term in Afghanistan when a land mine went off close to him. He had a metal plate for that and a lot of face damage. That's how he ended up with those scars. It wasn't long until he was diagnosed with PTSD."

"PTSD?"

"It's Post-Traumatic Stress Disorder. It's something a lot of people get after they've had a lot of stress, especially if they're in combat. Most PTSD people need help, so Randy went to Ramirez. I was working there at that time. Knowing he was more important than college didn't take me long. The next thing I knew, we were married.

"After a short time at the Army Health Clinic, Doctor Ramirez left the military and changed his practice to child psychology. He came here. I guess you could say Randy and I just followed him. Then we bought our house here and met you and Michael."

"We don't see much of Randy. How is he doing?"

"He has good days and bad days. His head injury healed, and his facial scars faded somewhat, but his PTSD didn't. He prefers being alone. That's another PTSD thing. Thanks to Michael, he got his job. It means a lot to him. Anyway, he'll be on the road tomorrow, so I'll be home alone. Andrew would be good company for me."

*   *   *

It was early morning when Ellen brought Andrew to Maya's house. "He already had breakfast, and we should be back before noon. Now you behave, you hear," Ellen said as she hugged Andrew.

"You goin' to that doctor place?" Andrew asked.

"Yes, we're going to see Doctor Ramirez."

Andrew wrapped his arms around his mother. "Mom, are you sick?"

"No, Andrew. I'm just fine. He just wants to talk to your dad and me about some things."

"What kinda things?"

"Just doctor things."

Andrew's jaws tightened as he pulled away from Ellen. "Crazy things! Crazy things about me, I bet."

Maya bent over and lifted Andrew's chin. "No one thinks you're crazy, Andy. The doctor just thinks you might be worrying over some things a boy your age shouldn't be concerned about."

Ellen kissed Andrew on the forehead. "I promise I won't

be gone long. We'll go to the park for a while when I get back. Then we'll come home and let you open your birthday presents. Then you can go trick or treat, okay?"

Andrew shook his head. "No, I just want to go back to my house."

Ellen looked at Maya. "Can you watch him at our house?"

Maya nodded, "Sure, if he's more comfortable there." After Ellen left, Maya took Andrew into the kitchen. "I can make you a cake if you want. What's your favorite?"

"Chocolate, but my Mom always makes me one for my birthday. It's always a chocolate cake. She knows that's my favorite. I'll bring you a slice if you want me to."

"I would love to have some, but it makes my sugar get too high."

"What does high sugar mean?"

"It's called diabetes. That means I need to take medicine to keep it normal."

"Will the cake make me have it too?'

Maya laughed. "No, Andy, but if you have it, you have to be careful what you eat."

"My name is Andrew."

"Sorry about that, but you are Andy to me."

Andrew nodded. "I guess Andy's okay. Tell me what happens if you don't take your medicine."

"Well, you can get sick . . . very sick. But I'm careful. I check my glucose every day-"

"Glucose? What does that mean?" Andrew asked.

"It means sugar. I check my sugar every day, so I know how much insulin I need to take."

"What's insulin?"

"It's sugar medicine. I take a shot, and then I'm good for the rest of the day."

"Show me how you take the insulin stuff."

"Okay," Maya said as she opened the refrigerator door and took out a small bottle then a tiny syringe from the kitchen cabinet. "This is the insulin. I just put this needle into the bottle and draw out how much I need, and then I stick the needle in my belly."

"Can I do it?"

"Can you do what?"

"Can I fill the syringe and shoot you with it?"

Maya laughed. "I guess you can shoot me with it. Just pull this up until the insulin gets to here," she said as she handed him the bottle of insulin and a syringe. "But *shoot* me in the back of the arm instead of my belly."

"I have the sugar medicine in the syringe," Andrew said. "Now, what do I do?"

"Wipe my arm with this alcohol pad, push the needle into my arm, and push out the insulin. That's all there is to it."

"Will it hurt?"

"Just a sting sometimes, but go ahead, and then we can go to your house."

Andrew watched as Maya flinched when the needle went

into her arm, then he handed her the empty syringe. "Can we go to my house now?"

"Sure, I rented a movie I think you'll like," Maya said as she put the insulin bottle back in the refrigerator and tossed the used syringe into the garbage.

* * *

While Doctor Ramirez was waiting for Ellen and Michael, he scanned Andrew's test results. The results were confusing. One study suggested one thing, another something else. One even supported Andrew being normal. He dismissed that one. Maybe Andrew was not crazy, but he was not normal.

"Doctor Ramirez is waiting for you," Kelly said as she took Ellen and Michael to Ramirez's office. When they entered his office, Ramirez shoved the previous study results aside.

"Have a seat, and we'll go over the test results." His tone and the sullen look on his face told Ellen something was wrong.

"What do the studies say?" Michael asked as he held his wife's hand.

"Nothing that points to any specific diagnosis."

Ellen relaxed. "So nothing is wrong?"

"I didn't say that, Mrs. Barlow. Something is wrong, but I just don't know what it is. One test answer goes in one direction; another goes in another. But what troubles me the most are the pictures he drew and things he said he saw under hypnosis."

Ellen stood up. "What do you mean by *you don't know?* Is my son is mentally ill or not? You're the-"

Michael eased her back into her chair. "Honey, let the doctor finish. I'm sure he has some opinion," then he looked at Ramirez. "What troubles you, Doctor?"

"First, let me ask you a few questions. I asked you once if you had another child. If you remember, all you said was that he was dead. You didn't want to go any further than that. But Andrew might have overheard you discussing the issue at home. He might not have understood what he heard, but he would have seen that it worried. That would have started him to worry about it."

The Barlows looked at each other. "We always tried to make sure he wasn't listening, but-"

"Children pick up on words and looks, so it's hard to know what they hold on to," Ramirez said. "But let me tell you about the hypnosis." He opened Andrew's file and pulled out a colorful drawing. "This is what he drew when I asked him to draw a picture of him and his family." He handed the drawing to Ellen. "What do you see there?"

Ellen looked at the drawing. Then with a confused look on her face, she handed it to Michael. "There are two boys between Ellen and me," Michael said as he looked at Ramirez.

"At first, there was just him, but when he started to show it to me, he suddenly pulled it back and started drawing again." Seeing the looks on their faces, Ramirez said, "I'll ask you again about the child that died. It seems to be important to Andrew."

Grabbing Michael's hand again, tears built up in Ellen's eyes. She took a deep breath and went back to the twelve-year-old horror. After she finished telling Ramirez things she kept buried in her mind, she wiped the tears from her cheek. "All Andrew knows is that he had a brother that died. We never went into the details. How could he-"

"I need for you to go into details with me. It might give me something to work with."

Ellen nodded as he looked at Michael. "Go ahead, tell him."

Michael hesitated while he plunged through years of memories, most good, some bad, but the few bad ones overshadowed the good ones. "Not sure where to start," he said as he looked at Andrew's drawing again. "I guess it started with Andrew's birth. Ellen was pregnant with him shortly after we settled here. Being new to the area, we hadn't found a doctor for her.

"Mrs. Collins was not only a good neighbor; she was also a good midwife. Since Mrs. Collins was just a house away, I went to her. Problem solved, so I thought. It turned out that a *breech birth*.

"Other than knowing it wasn't normal, I had no idea what a breech birth was. Mrs. Collins said she had some experience with this type of delivery, so I didn't need to worry." Michael hesitated again, took a deep breath, and then looked at Ellen. She gave him a nod. "When Andrew was finally here, I figured everything was okay."

During another long pause, Ramirez spoke. "You said there were twins. What happened to the other child?"

"It's difficult to explain, Doctor, but I'm getting there. Just give me a minute. What came next was something Mrs. Collins never experienced."

Tears ran down Ellen's cheeks. "Go on, honey. Tell him what happened."

Michael hid his face in his hands and took a deep breath. After he regained his posture, he continued. "I can only tell you what I saw and what Mrs. Collins told me. While Mrs. Collins cleaned Andrew up, something else came out of Ellen. The look on Mrs. Collins' face told me it was something that shouldn't be there. She knew I saw it too. I was too startled to ask questions. All I could think of was the flattened, paper-thin, parchment-like fetus that should have been a baby. It was clear that she didn't want Ellen to see what she put in the pan. She called it a Fetus something or another."

"It's often called *vanishing twin,* mainly because there's not much else you can call it," Ramirez said. "It's there, and then it's not. I guess *underdeveloped* might be a good word as any, but-"

Seeing the stress on Michael's face, Ellen put her arm around him. "Mrs. Collins never told me anything about the birth," she said, "but when Michael was walking her home, he pushed her until she explained it to him, or at least try to explain, what had happened-"

Ellen's tears were building up again. After wiping away her tears again with a tissue, Michael squeezed her hand and continued. "Mrs. Collins said that sometimes with twins, one of the fetuses could be absorbed by the mother or squeezed to death and sucked up by the other fetus, without anyone ever knowing it happened, not even the mother. But she had never seen or heard of one growing as big as this one."

"So Mrs. Barlow was pretty much in the dark at that time?"

"I guess you could say that, and Ellen had already suffered enough. Mrs. Collins said there wasn't anything we could do, so I decided not to tell her all of the details. But after thinking about it for a while, I decided, developed or not, she would want us to handle the twin as we would if he was normal, so I finally told her.

"She took it pretty hard, you know, feeling guilty and all, but Mrs. Collins gave her a stern lecture about *sometimes things just happen*. Bless her soul. She had a way to ease the pain. So, we decided to have a proper funeral for the baby. We named him Jimm Barlow II after my father and buried him in the graveyard on Shadow Lane."

"Did Andrew ever know about this, about *it*?" Ramirez asked.

"The other baby was never an *It*!" Michael said sharply.

"But no, we never told Andrew any details other than that he had a brother who had died."

Seeing the anger in her husband's face, Ellen reached for his hand. "It's okay, honey," she said as she looked back at the doctor. "I'm sure Andrew didn't know anything about his brother."

"But he might have?" Ramirez said.

Ellen shrugged her shoulders. "I guess he could have heard Maya and me talking, but we were always careful about the words we used and made sure Andrew was not close."

Ellen continued looking at Ramirez. After a minute of quietness, Michael broke the silence. "Since *you* know all the details, tell us what this has to do with what Andrew is going through."

"It's not always what you hear that drives you," Mister. Barlow," Ramirez said. "Just seeing anger, fear, or other facial expressions can be just as embedded in your mind." He waited a minute to let his words soak in. There was no reaction. "Okay, let me tell you about the hypnosis session."

After hearing the results of the hypnosis, Ellen and Michael left the doctor's office unsure about what they saw, unsure their son might have overheard a conversation about a dead, unformed fetus. The drive home was quiet until they saw the ambulance in their driveway. "Oh my God!" Ellen shouted.

CHAPTER XI

Ellen and Andrew arrived at the hospital just as they took Maya into the emergency room. It was clear to Ellen that she was still unconscious.

"Are you family?" the attending nurse asked.

Ellen shook her head. "No, just neighbors, but we're good friends."

"What do you know about her health?"

"Not much, but I'm not aware that she has any major medical problems. What do you think happened? Was it a heart attack?" Ellen asked as she followed the stretcher towards the emergency room.

"It doesn't look like a heart issue," the nurse said.

"Then the only other thing I can think of is her being diabetic, but she keeps it in control with a few units of insulin."

"Well, we won't know for sure if that's her problem until the doctor examines her and runs some tests. There's a waiting room over there. I'll let you know how things are going."

While Ellen and Andrew were snuggled together in the waiting room, a woman and a man approached them. The woman in tight trousers, a buttoned-up shirt, and a navy blue jacket looked familiar. Ellen remembered seeing her before but wasn't sure when. However, she had never seen the tall, thin man before.

As the two came closer, she remembered where she had seen the woman. When she saw the golden badge clipped on the woman's waist and the gun partly covered by her coat, she remembered who she was.

"Mrs. Barlow, you might not remember me," Jessica Marten said, "but we met a few years ago when I was investigating an accident in your neighborhood."

It took Ellen a few minutes before her concern over Maya faded enough to answer. She nodded. "Yes, I remember you now—the Ricardo boy's accident. You were in a police uniform then. Did you know his father committed suicide after that?"

"Yes, I heard about that," Detective Marten answered. "Do you still live on Shadow Lane?"

Ellen nodded. "We're thinking about leaving, but you know, thinking and doing aren't always the same."

"I know how that is. I thought about leaving the police department at times, but I decided to stay when they promoted me to Detective," Marten said. "This is my partner, Detective Jason Bradley."

"What brings you here?" Bradley asked. "I hope no one in your family is sick."

"It's our neighbor."

Marten narrowed her brow and looked at her partner,

then back at Ellen. "Any chance your neighbor would be Maya Jackson?"

"Yes. How did you know?"

"We answered the 911 call from someone in the Lane that said there was someone unconscious. My partner and I went to the hospital to see who it was, and if possible, find out what happened."

"She was babysitting our son when-"

Andrew quickly interrupted. "Mom, she wasn't *babysitting* me. She was just visiting."

Ellen forced a smile. "Mrs. Jackson was just *visiting* while my husband and I were going to a doctor's appointment."

Both Detectives laughed. "Andrew, you are a lot bigger than when I last saw you," Marten said. "And I hope your friend gets well."

"When I saw her get sick," Andrew said with a look of pride on his face, "I got scared at first, but I remembered what Mom told me about dialing 911 on the phone if there was a problem and someone would come over. So I called the 911 number and told the lady that answered that someone seemed to be sick. She asked a lot of questions I didn't understand, so I hung up the phone and sat down next to Mrs. Maya while I waited for the ambulance to come."

Marten answered with a wide smile. "That was very smart of you."

"Well, I did know she had a sugar problem. She told me she had to take her sugar medicine to make the sugar go down. Then she showed me how to put the sugar medicine in the needle, and then she let me put the needle in her arm."

Marten narrowed her brow as she looked at Ellen. "Is that right, Mrs. Barlow?"

"Yes, she is a diabetic, but I don't know about her showing Andrew how she takes her insulin or letting him give it to her."

"In Mrs. Collins' house?"

"Yes, Mrs. Collins's house. I guess you could say we replaced one good friend with another. We knew we could always depend on Maya. Anyway, we asked her to watch Andrew while my husband and I went to go over some of Andrew's tests with his doctor."

Marten looked at her partner then back at Ellen. "How did the studies turn out?"

"Just a childhood thing," Ellen said as she smiled at Andrew. "Nothing to be worried about."

Remembering the past malice on Shadow Lane, Detective Marten raised an eyebrow then sat down next to Andrew. "So, it was just you and Mrs. Jackson at your house?"

Andrew grinned. "We were at her house first, but she had a movie she thought I would like. I wanted to watch the movie, but her TV was small, so we went to my house. My TV is bigger than she has."

"It's nice to have friends like that," Marten said as she looked at her partner again.

Bradley patted Andrew's shoulder. "And she was lucky that you were there, you know, saving her and all."

"Detective Bradley's right, Andrew," Marten added. "That was very brave of you. So Mrs. Collins was at your house when she got sick?"

"Yes, ma'am. She was reading a magazine while I watched the movie. It was a kid's movie. It wasn't a very good one, so I went into the kitchen to get something to drink-"

"Did Mrs. Jackson look okay when you went into the kitchen?"

"She was just sitting on the couch like she always does, but when I came back, she was lying on the couch with her magazine on the floor. I thought she was just sleeping, but when I couldn't wake her up, I got scared and didn't know what to do. Then I heard the siren. A doctor person put his hand on her neck and then put the thing around his neck on her chest. Then they put her in the ambulance and left. But one stayed here with me until my parents got here. But I knew something bad had happened."

"Well, you were the hero today," Bradley said. "And she was lucky, very lucky that you knew what to do."

As the Detectives were about to leave, the nurse came into the room. "Mrs. Barlow, Mrs. Jackson is going to be okay. Her glucose level was dangerously low, but it only took a few glucagon injections to bring her out of her coma. It was a close call, though," she said as she put her hand on Andrew's shoulder. "If it wasn't for this boy here, it's likely she would have died."

Detective Marten was quiet as they left the waiting room. Her partner could see something was troubling her. "What's on your mind, Jessica?" her partner asked.

"It just doesn't make sense. This woman has used insulin for several years, and all of a sudden, she overdoses with it." As she reached the door to leave the hospital, she stopped and turned around. "I want to talk to the ER."

Doctor Sanders was just leaving Maya's room when the two detectives met him. "Are you Maya Jackson's doctor?" she asked.

"Yes, at least while she's in the emergency room, but the nurses are getting her ready to go to another room where she'll have another doctor."

Marten flashed her badge again. "I'm Detective Marten, and this is my partner, Detective Bradley. We have a few questions about Mrs. Jackson if you have the time."

Glancing at his watch, the doctor nodded. "What do you want to know?"

"The nurse said she took too an overdose of insulin," Marten said, "but that doesn't sound-"

"I don't know how it sounds to you, Detective," Sanders said as he looked at his watch again, "but it didn't take long to see she had overdosed on her insulin. I need to get back to work, so do you have any more questions?"

"So you're sure it was just diabetes and not a heart attack or a stroke?" Marten asked.

"I guess you could say it was her to diabetes since her blood glucose was deadly low, and as I said, the only way that could happen would be if she took an overdose of insulin. Only a rapid glucose IV saved her."

Marten looked at her partner, then at the doctor. "I don't understand. Wouldn't she have known she was in trouble?"

"Not necessary. Considering the amount of insulin she had, the glucose level would have dropped to a dangerous level. It would have happened slowly with only minor symptoms like dizziness and fatigue. Gradually she would have drifted off into an unconscious state that she would never come out of."

"So you think it was just an accident?"

The doctor took a deep breath and shook his head. "That's another story, Detective. I understand she has been using insulin for several years, but just to be sure, I called her doctor. He agreed she knew how much she needed each day."

"And how much was that?"

"Based on her A1C test-"

"A1C? What is that," Bradley asked.

"The A1C shows the average glucose level over a few months. Although it wasn't normal, it was relatively low for a person with diabetes. Her doctor said she only needed a low dose of insulin in the morning, something like ten or twelve units."

"That sounds like a lot," Bradley said.

"It might sound like a lot, but it's not. It's just a fraction of what she had to take to get so close to dying. But as far as knowing if it was an accident or a suicide attempt, I can't say."

"But it could have been a suicide attempt?" Marten asked.

"Suicide attempt or accident? I can't say. That's your field, Detective."

"Wish we could get our answer with a blood test."

"You're in the wrong profession for that," Sanders said in an irritating tone, "but suicide? I'm not a policeman, but it seems pretty clear to me that if she did it intentionally, you would think she would have done it at home instead of in front of the little boy she was watching,"

"That's a good point, Doctor," Marten said. "Can we see her now?"

"If you need to, but I don't think she'll be up to answering any questions."

"How long will she be here?" Marten asked.

"We're going to discharge her tomorrow if she has someone at home to keep an eye on her."

"Her neighbor out there said her husband works for him, and he'll give him a couple of days off to be with her," Marten said.

"Well, for now, she needs her rest, so don't stay long," the doctor said just as the overhead speakers announced, *Doctor Sanders needed in the ER.* "That's for me. I have to get back to work."

The detectives looked at Maya sleeping with a liquid dripping into her arm. It was clear she couldn't give any answers to their questions. Bradley looked at Marten and asked, "Where do we go from here?"

"We go back to the past."

"What do you mean by *going back to the past?*"

CHAPTER XII

THE SATURDAY BEFORE HALLOWEEN, ANDREW DECIDED he wanted to be a Vampire. After trying on his Vampire cape and makeup, he went into the backyard to see what Growly was barking about in the backyard as he always did when it was getting dark. "Guess you want to come into the house," Andrew said as Growly snuggled up against his leg. Andrew patted the dog's head then said, "Can't now, but maybe later." Then he shouted, "Ouch!" as blood ran over his wrist. "Why did you do that, Growly?"

> *Go on with your trick or treating. I'll stay with Growly. We need to spend some time together anyway. I'll teach him not to bite too.*

An hour later, Andrew was home picking out the best candy from his plastic pumpkin.

Ellen grabbed one of his chocolates, then gave lipped a false, *sorry!* As she unwrapped the candy, she realized how quiet it was outside. "Is Growly still outside?" she asked.

"Oh, I forgot. I told him I'd bring him in after I came back home. I'll go get him." Minutes later, Andrew came crying as he ran into the house. "Mommy, the gates' open, and Growly ain't out there. Someone must have stole him."

"You probably forgot to close the gate, and he wondered off. Don't worry; he'll be back when he gets hungry."

A week past, and Growly had not come back home. When Michael went into the shed out back, he saw why.

That night, in the attic, Andrew was silent. *He* wasn't.

Sorry about our dog; he kept barking. I tried
to shut him up, but maybe I hit him too hard.

*　　*　　*

Detectives Marten and Bradley were back at their desks scanning the files of all the deaths that occurred on Shadow Lane over the past ten years. Of the twenty-five deaths, thirteen were considered natural deaths, six due to illness, and three by accidents: two of which were by cars and the other by falling off a ladder while cleaning the house gutter. That left the three deaths that troubled Marten: Olivia Collins falling down attic stairs, Billy Ricardo hitting his head on a tombstone, and David Ricardo's suicide.

She put all of the documents aside except three. She shoved them toward Bradley. As if she didn't already know the answer, she asked, "What do these three have in common?"

Recalling the story Marten told him about her first visit with Mrs. Collins. Bradley was quick to take advantage of the *Melissa* story. "I guess you could make it four . . . if you count the cat."

"Very funny, Detective, but we still don't count cats," Marten replied as she held back a laugh.

"Besides being dead," Bradley said with a grin, "just what do they have in common.

Marten didn't find him funny. Instead, she answered him with a contemptuous look.

"Sorry, Boss," Bradley said. "First, they all lived on Shadow Lane. Secondly, they all lived just a few doors away from the Barlow family, but that doesn't tell us much."

"You're right, genius. It might just be a coincidence, but I think we need to take another look at the files on these three and talk to Mrs. Jackson again."

"You don't think they were accidents?"

Marten took a deep breath. "I'm not sure, but we might have a serial killer on our hands."

*　　*　　*

The two detectives were waiting at the funeral home when Carl Swartz arrived in his two-year-old Cadillac, wearing a white shirt, a black tie, and a black two-piece suit. At age forty-two, his short hair was already turning gray while wrinkles began deforming his face, and he walked with a cane. However, he was able to hide these faults of nature from his customers with the magic of his profession.

When Swartz saw the young, well-dressed couple standing by a new model car waiting for him, he assumed they were customers. He smiled while the price of an expensive coffin and tombstone, things young people always wanted for their departed *loved ones,* even if they couldn't afford them, ran through his head

As he walked from his Cadillac, he put on his mournful face. "I'm Mister Swartz," he said as he removed his black Fedora hat. "I would like to say, *it's glad to see you,* but under the circumstances, that would be-"

Marten interrupted him. "Mister Swartz, I'm Detective Marten, and this is my partner, Detective Bradley."

Swartz's mournful look quickly changed to one of concern. "Detectives, what can I do for you?"

"Can we go inside?" Marten asked. "We want to get your opinion on some of the . . . some of the people you *served.*"

"I hope this doesn't take long," Swartz muttered as he brought the detectives to his office. "I've got a family coming soon."

"We won't take much of your time, sir," Bradley said. "We just have a couple of questions."

Swartz listened to the detectives' questions, then answered them. "I care for those who pass away, Detectives, but I don't question how they died. That's your and the Medical Examiner's field, but as tragically as they were, all of these deaths on Shadow Lane seemed to be due to old age or accidental."

"You might be right, Mister Swartz," Marten said. "But since you take care of a lot of deaths in Savannah, most of which are on Shadow Lane, we thought you might have seen something unusual with some of them, something the recent Medical Examiner might have missed."

"Detective, people die, young, old, and for a lot of reasons," Swartz said with a rasped tone.

"You're right," Marten grunted, "but I still have some doubt that all of the deaths we're investigating were natural deaths."

"Detective, I'm an undertaker, not a Medical Examiner or a detective. I just fix them up to look good for their loved ones; then, I send them to wherever the family wants them to go. By the time I get them, folks like you and the Medical Examiner have already decided if their death was natural or not. I suggest you talk to the new Examiner if you have any questions. His name is Louis Redman."

"Just one more question," Bradley said. "You've been here how long, fifteen years or so?"

"Yes, eighteen years to be exact, Detective."

"And how long have you known Mrs. Collins?"

"I don't know what that has to do with your investigation, but she worked for me for a few years. Not in the embalming and prettying up part, mind you, but just office things. She didn't stay long, though, but then, no one does."

"Did you know her daughter, Rachel?"

"Rachel? Yes, I knew the child," Swartz said with a smirk on his face. "I arranged her funeral."

"Funeral arrangements?" Marten asked as she looked

at her partner, then back at Swartz. "I didn't know she was dead. What did she die from?"

"Some blood disease, Hemophilia, I believe," Swartz said. "She was about eight or nine when she died. Mrs. Collins didn't have anyone to look after her. That was one of the reasons she left me. The only thing I could do for her when the child died was arrange her funeral. I gave her a low price, a very low price!"

"I'm confused," Marten said. "She tells everyone that her daughter is in college and has a part-time job."

"Why would she lie about something like that?" Bradley asked?"

"She's not lying, Detective. She makes herself believe it. It's just like the dead cat she looks for every day. The poor woman's done that for years. Some people just can't accept losses, especially losing a young child."

*   *   *

Doctor Redman was in the process of an autopsy when Marten and Bradley arrived at his office. Once he finished closing up the corpse, he met the detectives in his office.

"It would be helpful if you gave us your opinion about how these people who died while living on Shadow Lane over the past few years," Detective Marten said as she laid the Collins and the Ricardo files on the medical examiner's desk.

"It sounds like you don't believe they were natural or accidental deaths," Redman said as he scanned the files. "I can assure you, Detective; Doctor Larson was competent in his work, so if-"

"We're not challenging Doctor Larson's work," Marten said, "but we just want you to look over the files and give us your opinion, that's all."

Redman began to show his irritation. "If anything looked suspicious, Doctor Larson would have picked up on it."

"I realize that everyone makes mistakes at one time or another," Marten said. "But two deaths closed as accidents, and a third wrote off as a suicide, all that victims who lived just a few houses apart from each other on Shadow Lane and died a year apart on the thirty-first of October each year, was a coincidence. That concerns us, but we would like your opinion."

Then there's the *accidental* insulin overdose this Halloween," Bradley added.

Redman raised his brow. "An insulin overdose?"

"You may not have heard about Mrs. Jackson," Marten said. "She's a long-time diabetic on insulin who suddenly makes a mistake and takes an overdose of insulin big enough to make her come close to dying."

Redman shrugged his shoulders. "I didn't know about her, but there was no reason for me to know since no one died."

Marten returned Redman's irritated tone. "Well, the police department thinks you should know about it!"

After being reminded that he worked for the enforcement

officers and others, Redman calmed down. "As you know, Detective," he muttered, "I haven't been here very long, and I never saw any of these people before or after their deaths, so I don't know any thins about these people."

"You have Larson's files. You can look over them, and you can talk with Maya Jackson," Marten said as she wrote down Maya's address.

Redman nodded. "I guess I can look over them, but I don't know how much that will help you."

Redman spent the night thinking about what the Detectives said. After a sleepless night, he decided to call his predecessor, Doctor Louis Larson.

"Doctor Larson, my name's Louis Redman. I took your old job as Medical Examiner. I hate to bother you, but I would like your opinion on some of the deaths in the Shadow Lane neighborhood of the city over the past several years."

After a half-hour conversation, Doctor Larsen grumbled, "A suicide is a suicide, and an accident is an accident. I didn't do a complete autopsy because there weren't any signs or evidence of foul play. Had they been, I would have been on top of it, Louis. There's not much more I can tell you."

A few hours after Redman's telephone conversation with his colleague, Larson, Detective Marten knocked on the Jackson's door. "Sorry to bother you, Mister Jackson," Marten said when Randy opened the door. "But we would like to talk to Maya again."

Randy was irritated with most people, one of the

emotional effects of PTSD; talking to two detectives was no different. "Haven't you had enough time to *fill in the blanks?*" he shouted with an angry outburst. "Can't this wait?" he asked. "She just came home from the hospital. Besides, she's sleeping right now."

Seeing the abrasive look on her partner's face, Marten was quick to take control. "I know we've spent a lot of time with her; that can be irritating, but we want to make sure-"

"Make sure it wasn't a suicide attempt?"

"Mister Jackson, we just want to see how she's doing," Marten replied in her soft voice, "and we want to be sure it was an accident and not . . . well not something someone else was involved in."

"You don't think I had anything to do with it, do you? I wasn't even here."

Beginning to share her partner's irritation, Marten gave Randy a frown and a glare. "Of course not, Mister Jackson, all we want to do is to-"

Hearing her husband's loud voice, Maya quickly came to the door. "Randy, go back to the book you're reading and let me talk with the detectives."

As usual, after an outburst, Randy rubbed his face and nodded. "Sorry, Detectives, but I'm just as upset over what Maya went through."

After Randy went back into the house, Maya invited the detectives into the living room. "Randy doesn't usually get this angry, but sometimes his PTSD gets in his way and . . .

well, he doesn't mean any disrespect. What do you want to ask me?"

Marten revisited what they already knew. "So you were alone with Andrew, and you let him inject your insulin, is that right?"

"Did you fill the syringe, or did you let Andrew do that?" Bradley asked.

"I'm not sure. What happened before I passed out is a little fuzzy. But Andy's a good boy. He was worried about what he called my *sickness*. I didn't want him to worry, so I explained what diabetes was and how it was treated."

"Mrs. Jackson, you've been taking insulin for years. You know the dose to take. It had to be Andrew who drew up the insulin and injected it. He's a pretty smart boy, Mrs. Jackson. I can't see how he could have made that big of a mistake."

"You think he did it intentionally?" Maya said with a shake of her head. "No! It was an accident. He would never do that on purpose. It was my fault

The detective's next visit was with the Barlows again.

*   *   *

"I'm not sure what I can do for you," Ellen said as she invited the Detectives inside. "And I don't know why you need to talk to Andrew again."

"We just want to make clear what happened when Mrs. Jackson was babysitting . . . I mean *visiting*," Marten said when she saw Andrew coming into the room.

Ellen took Andrew by his hand and sat him down on the sofa. "Andrew, they want to ask you some more questions about when you were with Maya." She then turned to Marten. "Please, make it quick and be quiet. Michael is not feeling well and is in bed."

"We will, Mrs. Barlow. Sorry about Mister Barlow. What seems to be his problem?"

"It's a lung thing. Something he got working in the Ohio coal mines."

Marten turned her attention to Andrew and what happened before Maya went into the hospital. "She told me about her diabetes," Andrew said. "She said it wasn't something I could catch from her. Anyway, I hope I never get it. After she showed me how to use her medicine, I pulled the syringe thing to what she called the-" He stopped and thought for a minute then continued, "I think she called it the ten line . . . yea, that was it, the *ten unit* line . . . I think that was how much she said she used."

"Somehow, she got a lot more than the ten units, Andrew," Marten said. "Can you explain that?"

"No. I just pulled the syringe thing up to the ten mark line."

"Then how did it get enough to send Mrs. Jackson to the hospital?" Bradley asked.

Andrew's breathing began to be deep and fast. "I don't know. Maybe someone else pulled it more."

Marten looked at Ellen then back to Andrew. "I'm

confused, Andrew. You said you were the only one there with Mrs. Jackson."

Andrew's speech slowly decayed into chaotic repetition. "It wasn't . . . It wasn't . . . It wasn't . . . It wasn't . . ."

Marten put both hands on his shoulder. "It wasn't what, Andrew?"

Ellen pulled Andrew out of Marten's grip. "Can't you see he's confused with all of your questions?" Then she turned to Andrew. "Go to your room, honey, and calm down. Everything is going to be okay." Once he left, she pointed to the door. "You have asked all the questions you need to ask, so please go."

"Mrs. Barlow, he's trying to tell us something."

"I said please leave, Detective!"

"What now?" Bradley asked as they headed to their car.

Marten's frustration was clear. "The Medical Examiner's office is our next stop."

Ten minutes later, Doctor Redman's phone rang. Thirty minutes after that, Detectives Marten and Bradley were in his office.

CHAPTER XIII

DOCTOR REDMAN WAS WAITING IN HIS OFFICE WHEN Marten and Bradley arrived twenty minutes later.

"Sorry to bother you again," Detective Marten said, "but we have a few more questions to ask."

"Sit down, Detectives," Redman said as he pointed to his oak desk. "Like I said when you called, I just might have some answers for you. To start with, I called Doctor Larson, the previous Medical Examiner at the time of the deaths you're investigating. He said he didn't do full autopsies because he didn't believe they were necessary since the deaths were just what they appeared to be, two accidents and one suicide. When I compared the postmortem photos taken shortly after the deaths of Olivia Collins, David Ricardo, and Billy Ricardo, I agree with him, but–"

"So all Medical Examiners have to do is to look at bodies to decide there was no foul play?" Bradley asked in a tone that made it clear he was being critical rather than asking a question.

"There's a bit more to it than that, Detective," Redman replied as he pulled out the photos again. "I'm sure you detectives have missed a piece of evidence at one time or another. Anyway, Doctor Larson should have looked a little closer at the photos he had of each corpse, as well as the surroundings where they died."

"Maybe he was more focused on his upcoming retirement," Bradley said, again in his sarcastic tone.

Redman ignored him as he pulled out Mrs. Collin's photos. "This is why I said Doctor Larson should have looked a little closer at these photos," he said as he pointed to Olivia Collin's photo. "If you look closely at this photo, you can see that her alleged accident fall is questionable."

Both detectives stared at the photo. "I'm sorry, Doctor," Detective Bradley said as he scanned the picture again.

"It's like I said. Sometimes the obvious is not as obvious should be." Seeing that both detectives were confused, Redman laughed, something he rarely did and pointed to the top of the steps. "Look closely at the staircase; it has two banisters. Now this woman has gone up and down those stairs thousands of times over the years without falling, at least not as we know. Then look at the steps." He held up the photo again. "There are no obstacles on the steps to trip over."

"There are always accidents despite the safest environment," Bradley said.

Redman nodded in agreement. "Yes, Detective, that's true, but you didn't look close enough."

"I saw what you saw, Doctor; banisters and clear steps."

Redman handed the photo to Marten. "Is that all you see, Detective?"

Marten looked at the photo for only a minute and then handed it back to Redman. "One of her slippers is still at the top of the chairs."

"That would suggest what?"

Marten looked at her partner. "That suggests she fell from the top of the floor and not as she was going down the steps proving it wasn't an accident."

"Bingo! Detective," Redman shouted. "But accident or not, it's your problem now."

"What about the Ricardo photos?" Marten asked.

"Ah, we may have hit the jackpot with those two," Redman said as he pushed Olivia Collins' photo aside and pulled out David and Billy's photos.

What Redman pointed out in the postmortem photos made the detectives decide to revisit those they interviewed years ago. They started with Carl Swartz. When Swartz said he remembered something about the day Billy Ricardo died that might help them, it was enough for the detectives to believe the alleged accidental and suicide deaths were not what they appeared to be.

"It's on us now, Jason," Marten said as they left Redman's office. "It's time we looked at these deaths as murders."

* * *

Juvenile court judge, John McDowell, met with Detective Marten and her partner in his office. After listening to their case, he looked at his calendar. It will be a month before we schedule a hearing. If you come back with a little more evidence, I'll-"

Marten interrupted the judge. "Your Honor, we can't wait another month!" The urgency in her tone was apparent. "Halloween is just a few days away. If what we believe is true, we need to act now."

"I'll do my best to meet your agenda, Detective, but you can't push the court based on conjecture."

"Your Honor, this is not conjecture," Bradley said. "The Marlow boy was the last person to-"

McDowell stopped him with a wave of his hand and a sullen grin. "Detective, there's always someone to be the last one to see a victim *alive*. If it's a murder, the murderer is *usually* that last one. "Whatever you want to call it, believing the boy was *the last one* is not evidence, at least not enough evidence to drag a teenager into court. Get something more, and I'll get you your juvenile court hearing."

"Damn it!" Detective Marten muttered after they left McDowell.

"Calm down, Jess," her partner said as they drove back to their office. We still have a couple of days before the 31st."

"Jason, I'm not sure we can get what we need in that short period, especially if the Barlows keep us from talking to their son."

"Maybe we should go there again," Bradley said.

"I don't think it will be any good, but we don't have anything to lose."

"If we push her hard enough, maybe threaten to take the boy *downtown*, she might let us talk to him."

"We'll need the Judge's support to do that, and he won't give it."

"It's just a bluff, Jess. There's nothing to lose if she doesn't fall for it."

"Nothing but time, Jason, and we don't have much of that." Then she shrugged her shoulders. "Hell, it's worth a try, but let's go to the Jackson house first and put the Barlows last on our list."

*   *   *

Maya was still recovering when Randy answered the door. "Mister Jackson, I'm detective Marten, and this is my-"

"I know who you are, Detective. You're here about the Barlow boy again. Well, I don't know anything about him, and my wife has already told you all she knows about her accident."

"Some things have changed, Mister Jackson," Marten said, "so we need to see if your wife remembers anything more than what she told us. It won't take but a few minutes."

"We can do it here, Mister Jackson, or we can-"

Detective Marten cut Bradley off with a contemptuous look and then turned to Randy. "It'll only take a few minutes, and then we'll be gone."

Maya was in her bedroom when the detectives arrived, but she was close enough to hear what the detective was saying. She grabbed her robe and came to the door. "Randy, it's okay, honey, let them in."

"Mrs. Jackson, I'm sorry to-"

"It's okay, Detective. I remember you."

"Mrs. Jackson, I know we have talked before about Mrs. Barlow's boy, Andrew, but he keeps popping up."

"Popping up?"

"*Popping up* might not be a good word to use, but I don't know what other word to use, so let's just focus on your incident."

"We've been over this, Detective. It was an accident. I let him measure the insulin. I told him ten units. The syringe markings are pretty small, so I can see how he might have gone to the hundred marker line by mistake, you know, one-hundred units instead of ten. Like I told you before, it was just a mistake."

The detectives left with no more evidence than they had before. That sent them back to the Barlow's house again. When they pulled into 666 Shadow Lane, Detective Marten warned her partner. "Just let me do the talking, Jason. Down-down threats won't work with them. And if you come across with your *Bad Cop* attitude, they'll threaten legal action and toss us out the door."

* * *

Ellen was cleaning the attic when she saw the box of pesticides spilled on the floor. "How did this get knocked off the shelf? I told Michael to keep this stuff out of sight."She shook her head and exhaled as she stepped on a small stool and put the box of poison on the highest shelf. As she stepped back down, she saw two dead rats in the corner of the room. "Guess the stuff does work," she said with a squeamish look. As she was leaving the attic, the doorbell rang.

"Detectives, I told you not to hassle my son anymore," she said as she opened the door.

"Mrs. Barlow, we're just trying to tie up loose ends on some issues we have," Marten said. "We're hoping your son can help us."

"Andrew's told you all he knows, but if you insist, you can see him one more time. If you want to talk to him anymore after that, it will be with our attorney. Otherwise, please leave the boy alone."

"Where is he now, Mrs. Barlow," Bradley asked.

"He went to my neighbor's house, then he's going to see Pastor Garland."

"How long ago was that, Mrs. Barlow," Marten asked."

"About a half-hour ago. He should be back soon to go trick or treating."

"That's right; it's Halloween," Bradley said. "I guess he's getting ready for trick or treating early. Good idea, go early, get more."

"No, Detective, He went to give them some of the cookies he made. It's sort of like a reverse trick or treats."

"Is it okay if we come back later then?" Marten asked.

"I guess you can. Just don't spoil his birthday. He's thirteen years old today."

"I remember," Marten said. "His birthday and Halloween are on the same day. I should have brought him a present. What's he going to be this year?"

"He's going as a policeman. Now please excuse me. I have two rats to get rid of." Seeing the look on the two detectives' faces, she had to laugh. "No, not you! I have two real dead rats in the attic."

Back in their car, Marten hit the gas pedal.

"What's the hurry, Jess?"

"Other than Carl Swartz's statement, we haven't got anywhere with this investigation, Jason, so the *hurry* is to be sure he will be willing to testify about what he saw the day Billy Ricardo died."

* * *

Before going to see Pastor Garland, Andrew stopped at Maya's house. She wasn't home, so he left a half dozen of his homemade cookies in a small box on her porch and headed down the Lane to the West Side People's Church and Pastor Garland. The pastor was talking to his clerk when he got there. "Mister Andrew, I see you have joined the police now," Garland said when he saw Andrew. "I guess that keeps you too busy to come to Sunday school anymore."

"No, sir," Andrew said. "This is just a Halloween costume."

"It's been a long time since I've seen you and your mother. How is she doing?"

"She's doing okay."

"I'm glad to hear that. When she stopped coming to church all of a sudden, I was worried she might be sick, so I planned to stop by to see her. I guess you must be here, to . . . what's it called, trick or treat?"

"Kinda like that, but different. I decided to turn Halloween around and give treats instead of asking for them. That's why we brought you these cookies. I made them by myself. They're chocolate with nuts and sugar powder on top. I gave some to Mrs. Jackson next door to me."

"Why, thank you, Andrew. Although I don't believe in this Halloween thing, I do believe in cookies?"

"What's wrong with Halloween?"

"It's the devil's night, son. That's what it is. Those who celebrate the devil give away their soul. They no longer belong to God."

> *Remember what he said: 'Since this thing was not born alive, it doesn't have a soul and doesn't belong to God.'*

Andrew's voice became livid as his eyes turned into a predatory gaze. "I know! I remember."

Pastor Garland frowned. "What do you remember, son?"

Andrew's lips curled into a sneer as he blurted out: *Everything!*

"You sound scary, boy. Are you okay?" Garland snapped.

"It's Halloween, Pastor. Kids are supposed to be scary."

"Not when they dress up like Police Officers. Anyway, I appreciate the cookies. I'm getting ready to go out of town, and they'll be something to snack on."

"Hope you enjoy them. We made them especially for you," Andrew said with a grin as he turned and continued down the road swinging his empty plastic pumpkin.

*   *   *

On his way home, Andrew saw the two Detectives talking to Maya through the opened door on the porch. "What do you want to know now?" she asked the detectives.

"Sorry to keep bothering you, Mrs. Jackson, but we're just doing our job," Marten said.

"Yes, he brought me some cookies," Maya said. "It must have been earlier in the evening while I was gone. I thought it was nice of him to leave them on my porch, but I didn't eat any of them, you know, because of my diabetes."

After a few minutes of discussion, Marten realized Maya would not change her story about the insulin issue, so she turned the conversation back to the cookies. "Mrs. Jackson, be glad you didn't eat them. We think they may have been poisoned."

Mrs. Jackson laughed. "Poisoned! You must be kidding.

What would he know about poison, and why would he want to poison anybody anyway?"

"What would he know about insulin?" Bradley asked in his derisively attitude. "We think the cookies were tainted with-."

"We just want to have those cookies, Mrs. Jackson," Marten said as she shot Bradley her irritant look.

"What do you want with cookies you think were poisoned?"

"We'll give them to our toxicologist for testing; then we'll know for sure what's in them."

"I think you're wasting your time, but here they are," Maya said as she handed them the box of cookies. "Test them all you want. You might find a lot of sugar, but you won't find any poison."

The detectives headed to their van. Once there, Marten handed the box of cookies to her partner then rolled her eyes. "You can test them if you want, but not me!" Her tone revealed her frustration, something she usually left to her partner.

"She's going to stick to her story, Boss. She's just stubborn like most women," Bradley said. A quick slap on the back of his head followed.

"Stubborn maybe, but the question is if she really believes her overdose was an accident or is she trying to protect the boy?" Marten asked. "Either way, she's going to have a hard time explaining these cookies if the toxicologist finds they have what I think they have in them." Then she turned on the blinking lights and screeching siren. "I just hope we get to the pastor in time." Minutes later, they were pulling into the church's parking lot.

Mrs. Wilson was just closing the church when the detectives came rushing in for the evening.

"I'm Detective Marten, and this is my partner, Detective Bradley. We're here to see Pastor Garland."

"I'm sorry, but the Pastor isn't here right now."

"When will he be back?" Marten asked.

"You just missed him, Detective. He left for Pembroke half an hour ago. He goes there every week or so to see his brother. He's getting married tomorrow, and the Pastor's supposed to do his marriage ceremony. Is there anything I can help you with?"

"Did a boy give him some cookies?|"

Mrs. Wilson had a puzzled look on her face. "Cookies? Yes, the Barlow boy up the road brought him some cookies, why-"

"Did he eat any of them?"

"The pastor does have a liking for sweet things, so he probably did."

"How can we reach him?" Marten asked. "It's very important."

"I only know he went to see his brother in Pembroke. He usually stays there a couple of days when he visits. You might try his cell phone number," Mrs. Wilson said as she handed

Marten a card with the Pastor's number on it, but don't be surprised that he doesn't answer, he never does. "Other than that, you'll have to wait until he gets back."

As soon as they left the church, Bradley dialed the number Mrs. Wilson gave him. No one answered.

Marten took a deep breath and closed her eyes. "Let's drop this off at the toxicologist, then track down the Parson and hope afraid a couple of days won't be too late."

CHAPTER XIV

When Pastor Garland left Chatham County and entered Bryan County, he was two cookies and twenty minutes away from Pembroke when he began feeling weak. Stomach cramps and nausea followed. When he saw the *REST AREA NEXT EXIT* sign, he pulled in and called his brother.

"I'm not feeling good, Marshal . . . No, nothing serious, just cramps and some nausea. Probably just a virus, and I don't want to give it to you, so I'm going back to Savannah for the night, but don't worry, Brother, I'll be there in time for your wedding."

After ensuring his brother he would be there in time for his wedding, he called Mrs. Wilson. "Mrs. Wilson, just so you won't think someone is breaking into my house, I'm turning around and coming back tonight."

'What's wrong, Pastor?'

"Nothing serious. I don't feel good. It's probably just an upset stomach. I called my brother and told him I'd see him tomorrow."

"I just wanted you to know that two detectives came by to see you."

"Detectives? Did they say what they wanted?"

"They said they just wanted to ask you some questions."

"Questions? What questions?"

"*Other than asking if the Barlow boy gave you any cookies, they didn't say why or what. Since the cookies seemed important to them, I gave them your phone number.*"

"Why in the world would they care about a boy giving me a few cookies? You'd think they had more important things to do than worrying about cookies. Anyway, I ate most of them already."

"*Maybe I should call them and tell them you're on your way back.*"

"No, don't do that!"

"*Pastor, you're not in trouble with the law, are you?*"

"No, Mrs. Wilson, I'm not in trouble with the law. I just don't want them spending the day asking me questions that will keep me away from my brother's wedding."

"*I just don't want you to get in trouble with the police, but-*"

"I know, Mrs. Wilson, I know. But if they want to see me, they'll just have to wait until I come back from the wedding on Thursday."

"*I'm just your Associate, Pastor, but-*"

By this time, he was weak and dizzy. "We can talk about this later, Mrs. Wilson, but right now, I'm about to throw up." He was unsteady as he got out and leaned against the car. He took a shallow breath, vomited, and grabbed his chest a minute later. Pale and unresponsive, he fell to the ground.

His meeting with the detectives would never come.

* * *

As usual, Mrs. Wilson finished cleaning the church, arranged the pastor's list of *things to do,* and then settled down for the night to watch her favorite television series. Halfway through *Modern Family,* her sleeping pill took control and sent her drifting into a deep sleep. Then her phone rang.

"Is this Mrs. Wilson?"

"Yes, this is Mrs. Wilson. Who's calling me at-" she looked at her alarm clock, "at two o'clock in the morning?" The call in the middle of the night ran a chill down her back. A call from a State Trooper made it even worse. "Mrs. Wilson, this is State Trooper Norton down in Bryan County. Are you related to a man named Mister Ronald Garland?"

The voice on the other end of the phone tempered her irritation. "No, I'm not a relative; I'm just his Associate Pastor," she said. *Is he in trouble with the police,* ran through her mind?

"Does he have any family in Savannah?"

"No, but what's happened to him? Is he that sick?" She knew the answer before the patrolman could answer. In the pastoral business, *next of kin* meant only one thing.

"I hate to bring you bad news, Mrs. Wilson, but your pastor is dead."

Her chill changed to instant and clamant palpitations so

strong she could hear the throbbing of blood in her veins. All she could say was, "Oh, my God!"

"I know this is a shock to you, Mrs. Wilson, but they found the Pastor lying on the ground at a rest area an hour ago."

A long pause followed a deep breath. "How did he die?"|

"It looks like a heart attack," the trooper said. "Again, I'm sorry to have to break this bad news to you, but I need to contact his next of kin so we can know what to do with his body; you know, his burial or cremation. There were several names on his phone, but you were the last person he called, so I thought you might be a relative or know one of his relatives."

Mrs. Wilson broke down in tears. "He doesn't have any family here in Savannah, but he does have a brother in Pembroke. I think his name is Steven. Pastor Garland. He planned to do his wedding ceremony tomorrow, but Pastor Garland called me last night to tell me he wasn't feeling well, so he was coming back. The Pastor was a good man. How could this happen to him?"

"I understand how you must feel, Mrs. Wilson."

State Trooper Norton's next call was to Steven Garland, then back to Mrs. Wilson. "Mrs. Wilson, I contacted your pastor's brother. He wants the body brought back to Pembroke."

"Do they know when they'll have his funeral and when they're going to bury him? I need to know because there are a lot of people up here that will want to come to his funeral."

"His brother plans to have him cremated tomorrow and have a ceremony one day next week."

*   *   *

When Marten picked up the toxicologist's report, she had mixed emotions; one was satisfaction knowing she was right, the other, sadness knowing the evidence led to Andrew Barlow.

"Just like we suspected, Arsenic!" Bradley said as he looked at the toxicologist report over Marten's shoulder.

"Now, all we have to do is find Pastor Garland and hope we're not too late," Marten said as the thoughts about charging a thirteen-year-old boy with murder rambled through her head.

"And if he's already dead?"

"Then his autopsy can still tell us what killed him. Let's go back to see if he made it back home or not."

When they arrived back at the church, they found Mrs. Wilson on her knees praying. After finishing her prayer, she wiped the tears from her red eyes, turned to the two detectives, and shook her head. "If you want to talk to the Pastor, you're too late."

"Is he back at his brother's again?" Bradley asked.

"He never got there, to begin with," she said as she closed her eyes and began crying again. "He died early this morning."

"It looks like the poison beat us here," Bradley said as he looked at Marten.

"He wasn't poisoned, Detective. The man that called me said he died from a heart attack," Mrs. Wilson said in a bitter tone.

Marten decided not to argue the point. Instead, she put her arm around Mrs. Wilson. "I'm so sorry. I know how important the Pastor was to you and his congregation, but we need to contact his family and let them know we need to have an autopsy. That's the only way we will know for sure if it was his heart or if he died from poisoned cookies. But-"

"There won't be a body to test, Detective," Mrs. Wilson said as she buried her face in her hands. "He was cremated this morning."

Once the two detectives left Mrs. Wilson grieving, Detective Bradley shook his head, "There goes our case," he said.

"I know, we no longer have the solid case we wanted," Marten said, "but we still have the tainted cookies left at Mrs. Jackson's house." Detective Marten spent the night trying to find a way to have a thirteen-year-old boy put away for murder. Each time she would doze off, nightmares pulled her out of the little sleep her diazepam allowed. Finally, she looked at her alarm clock. "Damn it! It's two o'clock," she mumbled as she threw her pillow across the room.

Since she couldn't sleep, she grabbed a novel she started but never finished and cuddled up on the couch. When the sun rose, so did she. Ignoring breakfast, she dressed and met her partner.

"What got you up so early?" her partner asked when she got into the car.

"Lost evidence and nightmares, Jason."

"We still haven't lost our case yet, Jess," Bradley replied.

"Maybe, maybe not, but there's still these nightmares."

Jessica told Jason about her nightmares as they headed to the courtroom to meet with Judge McDowell again. "When I try to get his parents to talk about the Shadow Lane deaths and why we believe Andrew might be involved in them, Andrew comes in from nowhere shouting over and over, *Don't listen to her. It wasn't me who done it. She just don't like boys.*"

"What would you do if he was your son?"

Bentley paused for a minute, then, with a flustered look on her face, she continued. "Maybe it's a mother thing eating on me too when I ignore the evidence and tell myself that a nice boy like Andrew couldn't do the horrible things I think he did do. Then there are the nightmares!"

"We all have dreams, Jess. Even a hot male like me has them, but most of mine are about-"

"I'm not talking about your type of dreams, partner. Save them for the guys at the department. Mine are nightmares, crazy nightmares! Like when I'm talking to Andrew about his incompatible dilemma, I hear squeaking sounds then meanings. I look up to see all of the Shadow Lane dead people sitting up in their coffins staring at me. It scares the hell out of me sometimes."

"Then what?"

"Then I jump up sweating and take a shower."

*   *   *

Early the following day, the District Attorney and attorney Maria Bentley met with Judge McDowell in his office. The DA was still upset with the loss of evidence that would have supported his case, but he was more concerned about Andrew Barlow being free to commit more deaths. His only hope was that the judge would give the State some leeway. Without solid evidence, bringing a thirteen-year-old to court, even to a Juvenal Court, would be plastered all over the TV news and the newspapers. That would put the Judge's reelection in jeopardy. He could not let that happen.

"Your Honor," the DA said, "since they cremated the late Pastor Garland, the Staterealizes there's no evidence that this boy killed him." Then he glared at Bentley. "The State agrees with that, but there is evidence the boy wanted to kill Maya Jackson."

"That's just speculation, Your Honor," Bentley said.

"It's not *speculation*, Your Honor, Detective Bradley said in a bitter tone. "Leaving poison cookies for Mrs. Jackson to eat is proof that Andrew Barlow planned to poison her. At least, we can charge the boy with *intent to murder*. The evidence for that is not disputable."

McDowell nodded, "I agree with the District Attorney, counselor. I'll let this in *if* or when we go to trial."

Attorney Bentley slammed her hand on the table then jumped up. "Your Honor, the DA is putting the cart before the horse again, but-"

McDowell found it hard not to laugh. "Calm down, counselor. This isn't a Thanksgiving dinner discussion."

"Sorry, Your Honor. It's just that-"

McDowell's glare cut her off.

"What I meant to say, Your Honor, although the cookies *might* have been tainted with poison, there is no evidence that my client knew it."

The judge closed his eyes for a minute, then glared at her. "*Intent* to murder with *cookies?* The press will have a party with that."

"Your Honor, the boy murdered Pastor Garland and attempted to murder-"

Before Nelson could finish, the Judge stopped him with a raise of his hand. "Mister Nelson, I'm aware that it's frustrating for you, but the law requires more substantial evidence than what you have at this time. And a jury would want more too. As much as you want it to be true, I believe you would have difficulty proving your case. And here's another piece of advice. The late David Ricardo's death is still considered a suicide. I would be careful using the word *murder* so loosely. You might end up in front of me charged with the Barlows and a slander charge."

Nelson started to rebuke the judge. But the Judge's *you've said enough* stopped him.

After a minute of quietness, McDowell stood up. "Although the law says you have up to five days before you need to file a detention hearing, If the State plans to proceed with the Garland death, I'll consider today's conversation as your official complaint. But, before you file an official petition, you better have enough evidence to support it."

"Will you let Andrew stay at him until the trial?" Bentley asked.

"No. In consideration of the safety of the community, the Barlow boy will be in the custody of the Youth Detention Center," Judge McDowell said as he kept eye-to-contact with the DA. "But, unless the DA comes up with a strong *probable cause*, this will only be temporary, and I will send him back home. Remember, you only have seventy-two hours to file your charges from the time the boy goes to the Center, so I suggest you both burn the candle and get to work."

"Thank you, Your Honor," Nelson said. "I have reason to believe there's more evidence out there that will dispute the charges against Andrew."

CHAPTER XV

THE SAVANNAH LEDGER ASSIGNED THEIR REPORTER, Casey Carson, to follow the Andrew Barlow issue. Being new in the news business, Carson was eager to have the chance to have a front-page article. As usual, arresting detectives were the first people she wanted to give her a statement. However, the police policy prevented them from being dragged into speaking to press representatives about a pending crime.

Detective Marten and Detective Bradley held fast to that policy. Failing to get what she wanted, Carson decided to go elsewhere for her front-page story. *Elsewhere* was Maya Jackson and the Barlows.

"No, ma'am, Andrew Barlow would never do the horrible things they said he did. He's a good boy," Maya shook her head and continued, "Not my Andrew!"

"I know you think he's a good boy, but Mrs. Jackson," Carson replied, "but you almost died from an overdose of Insulin he put in a syringe. Then there's the cookies issue. There's little doubt he brought the poisoned pastries to you and the late Pastor Garland."

"I know, but I still don't believe he did those things intentionally."

"Mrs. Jackson, surely you-"

Maya ended the interview with, "Miss Carson, that's all

I have to say, so your newspaper needs to find someone else to give you a story."

Mrs. Jackson's interview didn't give the reporter the story she wanted. She hoped her interview with the Barlows would pay off.

Since Ellen and Michael did not have the money needed to hire an attorney, Judge McDowell appointed Maria Bentley to represent Andrew; Bentley was with the Barlows when Newswoman, Casey Carson, knocked on their door.

"Mister Barlow, my name's Casey, Casey Carson. I'm with-"

"I know, who you are, Miss Carson," Michael mumbled. "You're with the Savannah News. I've read some of your articles. I guess you're here to get an interview with our son."

"Yes, sir, I am," Carson said. I want to talk to Andrew, and then I'd like to hear from you about what you have to say about the things the District Attorney intends to charge him with. Then-" Before she could finish, Maria Bentley came to the door.

"Well, if it isn't my favorite reporter, Casey Carson," Bentley said. Then she turned to Michael. "It won't hurt to get our statements out to the public. What do you think, Mister Barlow?"

"If you think so?"

"I assume you'll be fair as usual," Bentley replied.

"Now, Miss Bentley, when was I ever not fair?"

"Let's see," Bentley said as she bit on her lip and scratched her head. "How about the Bryan Richard's murder when-"

Casey shook her finger at the attorney. "Richard's, huh? That's not fair, Maria. I might have danced around some *issues,* but-"

"So now it's *Maria,*" Bentley interrupted as she hugged her long-time friend. "She's okay, Mister Barlow, let the lady in."

Casey took a deep breath and chirped, "Finally, someone's willing to give the Post a statement,"

Casey was good to her word, and then some. When it came to an adult, the News' policy always sided with the public's side and the prosecution. But when it came to charges against a child, the public was always on the side of the defender. Maria made sure her article leaned in that direction:

> *Andrew Barlow lives next door to the woman who almost died from an overdose of insulin. Although the proposed victim denies the Barlow boy had any involvement in the incident, The District Attorney is likely to bring charges against the boy for attempted murder and other potential crimes. It is not clear what evidence the State has against the teenager.*

> *Young Andrew's Barlow's defense attorney, Maria Bentley, mocked the threat saying they*

are ambiguous and would never reach a jury.
Of course, that is yet to be determined.

She ended the article by going through the history and the hardships of the Barlow family. The next day her article was a front-page *Extra! Extra! Extra!*

*   *   *

"Why are all these people doing here?" Ellen asked as the Barlows entered the courtroom,

"Don't worry. They're just a bunch of nosey people who don't have a life of their own. I'll fix this," Bentley said as she strutted up to the judge's bench. "Your honor, can we have this hearing in closed session? After all, it's a thirteen-year-old we're going to hear about."

Judge McDowell nodded in agreement then tapped the bench with his gavel. "Bailiff, please empty the courtroom."

Mumbles and whispers filled the courtroom as dozens of disappointed people left, leaving only the judge, the Barlows, their attorney, Earl Nelson, and state-appointed social worker.

The Judge heard the State's position first.

"Your Honor," Nelson said as he pointed at Andrew, "the defendant, Andrew Barlow, is now thirteen years old. As you know, Georgia law states that teenagers accused of class A felonies can be tried as adults at the Court's pleasure."

Michael grabbed Bentley's arm. "My God! He *just* turned thirteen. Why-"

"Don't worry, Mister Barlow," Bentley whispered. "Just be patient and let the judge hear the charges the prosecuting attorney's going to present. Knowing what he's going to throw out is to our advantage."

Waving a finger at Andrew again, Nelson continued. "Your Honor, this defendant shouldn't be running free while he's waiting for a trial." Then the finger waved at the judge. "This hearing isn't even necessary, Your Honor. It's a waste of the court's time and the communities' money, besides-"

Bentley was quick to interrupt Nelson. "Your honor, other than my client living on the same street as the people who died, the state hasn't shown any proof that he did anything wrong. They have no evidence that he was even there when Mister Ricardo shot himself, or that he was in the cemetery when his son had his accident, or when Mrs. Collins fell down her steps. Even though rat poison somehow got into the cookies given to Mrs. Jackson and Pastor Garland, there is no proof that either of them ate any of them. All the DA has are presumptions."

"Your Honor, the defense is testifying, let-"

McDowell looked down at Nelson with a scalding look. "Mister District Attorney, it's my job to decide who's testifying and who isn't, what is necessary, and who is testifying. I suggest you use your time more appropriately and come back to me with hard evidence to support your charges."

When Bentley saw Ellen and Michael's concerned look, she leaned over and whispered to them. "Not only is the DA running against the judge in February, but he's also pissing him off. So just sit back and relax."

Seeing Bentley's wide grin, McDowell gave her an irritable glare. "And I don't need you, Miss Bentley, lecturing me about the law and telling me who has evidence and who doesn't."

"I'm sorry, Your Honor, if I got out of line, but what about the Barlow's son?"

"Oh, yes, the defendant," McDowell muttered. "It seems that between your and the DA's arguments, we forgot about him."

Although she knew the answer, Bentley asked, "Can he remain in his parent's custody for now?"

Nelson jumped up from his chair. "Your Honor, based on the seriousness of the charges, the defendant needs to be held in the State's custody."

The judge thought for a minute, then nodded. "I agree with the DA, Miss Bentley. For now, the boy will stay in the juvenile center in the custody of the State's Social Worker, Janice Willard, until I hear what crimes you plan to charge him with and what evidence you have to support those charges. Does everyone agree with that?"

"I agree," the DA said.

"And you, counselor?"

"Yes, Your Honor, the defense agrees."

Ellen looked at Miss Bentley and began to cry.

Then McDowell looked at his watch. "It's getting late, and I've heard enough for today. We'll adjourn until tomorrow at two o'clock." Then the gavel went down again. "Court is adjourned."

The Social Worker left with Andrew, while Ellen, tears ran down her cheeks, left with Michael's arms around her and Bentley and Andrew right behind them.

"It's going to be okay, Andrew," Ellen said as she looked back at Andrew.

Andrew looked back at his mother. Then he smiled. Only he heard the voice:

> *Don't worry; we're gonna be okay. They don't know nothin.*

*   *   *

When they arrived at the house where Andrew was to spend the night, he looked at the boys looking at him. Most were younger than him, a few older, all well dressed, and all curious about him.

"This is your room, Andrew," the staff manager, Mrs. Willard, said. "There's a closet over there where you keep your things. I don't know where your roommate is, but he'll be along soon to show you around. In the meantime, just rest." Then she left.

Andrew sighed as he tossed his small bag onto the bottom of the two-bed bunk bed that filled up one side of the room. On the other side, a door opened into a bathroom. Besides a small closet, a well-worn couch, a small side table, and a two-drawer dresser took up the other side of the room.

Suddenly the bathroom door opened. In the doorway stood a fat, shabbily dressed boy. After zipping up his pants, the boy slammed the door then glared at Andrew. "Get your shit off my bed!" the boy said as if he was the rooster in a hen house and Andrew was the hen.

Inside, Andrew was trembling; outside, he forced a smile. "Hi! I'm Andrew. Guess we have the same room."

The boy continued his glare as he strutted towards Andrew.

"Andy What?"

After a few steps, they were eye to eye. "I told you, my name's Andrew."

The boy tapped Andrew on the top of his head and grunted. "And I asked you, *Andy* what?".

Andrew backed away, partly because of fear, partly because of the boy's wretched smell. "I told you it's Andrew."

"And I said, *Andy what!*"

Don't let him push you around!

"It don't matter," Andrew grunted as he handed out his hand. "Andrew or Andy; It don't matter?"

The boy pushed Andrew's hand away. "That's more like it, *Andy*. It's best you know right off, I'm in charge here. Now get your shit off my bed."

Andrew backed off and tossed his bag onto the upper bed.

I said, don't let him push you around.

Andrew took a deep breath, closed his eyes, then muttered, "He's bigger than me, so don't make no trouble."

"What did you say?" the boy grunted as he pushed Andrew against the wall.

"I wasn't talking to you."

"You was talkin' to someone, with me bein' the only *someone* here. So you're either talkin' to yourself, or you're talkin' to me, *Freddy!Freddy* the Boss," he shouted as he made a fist and pointed it in Andrew's face. "And this is what makes me the boss around here. It's best you don't forget that!"

Andrew nodded. "I guess I was talking to myself."
"You *guess?* You a retard or something?"

"I'll only be here for tonight, Freddy, and I don't want to make no trouble, so let's be friends 'till I leave tomorrow."

"I don't need no friends retard." The fat boy's tone told Andrew he was trouble, just like Billy Ricardo.

You don't have friends 'cause you're stupid and fat.

"What did you say, Retard?"

"I didn't say nothin'," Andrew said.

"You must be asking for a whipping!"

Not by you, Turd-Head.

"Who you callin' a Turd-Head?"

> *Ain't nobody here but us, so I must be talkin'*
> *to you, PudgyRetard.*

Freddy's face turned red. No one had ever spoken that way to him. He had to stop it and stop it now, or he would lose the control he had fought for over the past year.

Freddy waved his fist in Andrew's face. "Nobody calls me fat or a Turd-Head!" A chill went down Andrew's back.

"I don't think you're fat, Freddy, and you're pretty smart too," Andrew said, hoping to calm Freddy down.

It worked. Freddy took it as an apology. "Then watch your mouth 'cause I am smart, and I'm pretty strong too."

"I'll be back in a minute," Andrew said as he gritted his teeth. "I gotta go to the bathroom."

"I orda' let you piss in your pants. Next time you call me names, that's what I'll do."

Once in the bathroom, Andrew took a deep breath. "You're goin' to get me in trouble, so just keep your mouth shut. I don't want to make him mad, so-" Before he finished his words, he looked into the mirror. His face changed from frightful pale to angry red as his eyes narrowed.

> *Don't you worry none. I know how to take*
> *care of fat idiots like him. He might push you*
> *around, but he ain't gonna do it to me.*

No longer in control, Andrew went back into the room

just in time to see Freddy climbing up the ladder to the top bed.

Why are you on our bed?

"Just lookin' in your bag to see if there's anything I might want," Freddy said as he tossed Andrew's clothes on the floor. "Nope, nothin' here but trash."

Leave our stuff alone, flabby ass!

Freddy's eyes widened in rage as he jerked Andrew closer to him. "Flabby ass?" Freddy barked. "You callin' me flabby ass? I'm gonna teach you a-"

Before Freddy could finish his threat, strong hands grabbed him by his shirt and jerked him off the bed onto the wooden floor.

I don't think he'll be any trouble anymore.

Andrew looked at Freddy spread out on the floor as a stream of blood flowed out of his head. "What have you done?" he yelled as he ran to the door. "Help! Help! Freddy got hurt!"

After the paramedics put Freddy in the ambulance, Mrs. Willard showed up again. "How is he doing?" she asked the paramedic.

"Alive," he said, "but he's in a coma."

"What happened to him?"

"You need to ask that boy over there. He was there when it happened."

Mrs. Willard took Andrew's hand, walked with him back to his room, and sat down on the bed with him. "Just what happened, Andrew?" she asked while still holding his hand.

"He just fell."

"Fell from where?"

"From the bed, I guess."

She pointed to the upper bed. "From up there?"

"I think so. That was supposed to be my bed, but Freddy wanted to change with me. I said it was okay, so he climbed up the ladder. Then he asked me what I had in my bag. I said nothing 'cept clothes. He looked into it anyway. When he saw I had nothing 'cept clothes, he tossed them down at me. Then I went to the bathroom. That's where I was when Freddy fell. When I came out, he was just laying on the floor." Andrew began to cry. "We were just making friends-it was all my fault?"

"No, Andrew, Freddy was a strange boy, always doing things he shouldn't do. So, no, it wasn't anyone's fault but him."

"Wow! Look at all that blood?" Andrew groaned.

"Do you think he's gonna be okay?"

"All we can do is pray he will," Mrs. Willard whispered. "All we can do is pray."

I pray he'll die!

"You pray he dies?" Andrew murmured.

Mrs. Willard jerked him by his shoulder. "What makes you even think I would pray for Freddie or for anyone to die?"

"No, ma'am, I didn't mean that."

"I sure hope you didn't."

"No, ma'am, I want to pray that he gets better," Andrew said as he cuddled next to Mrs. Willard. "Do you think they'll let me go home if we pray for that?"

Mrs. Willard smiled and hugged him. "We'll have to wait until tomorrow to see what God wants about that, Andrew, but we can surely while we pray. In the meantime, we don't need to tell anyone outside of the Center about Freddy's accident."

CHAPTER XVI

As Judge McDowell entered the room, the bailiff told everyone to rise.

After flipping through a list of papers, Judge McDowell called the defensive and the States attorneys to the bench. "The defendant's attorney asked for a bench trial, Mister Nelson. After deep thought, I agreed."

"Your Honor, if any charges deserve to be heard by a jury, these are," District Attorney Earl Nelson said. "I believe-"

McDowell raised his hand and cut Nelson off. "Mister Nelson, I respect the States' opinion but think about it. A jury of twelve, some likely to be parents, might lean towards the defense's argument. A judge will not let that affect his decision."

Judge McDowell saw the Post's Casey Carson as he looked at the audience. "I see the press is here on time, so watch your language." Loud laughter followed. "Quiet now," he said as he tapped the bench with his gavel. "Andrew Barlow is accused of a double murder, David Ricardo and Ronald Garland. We'll start with the Ricardo charge. The floor is yours, Mister Nelson."

Earl Nelson was known for his in-depth questioning, and now that he was running against the Judge sitting on the bench, he would be extra impeccable."

"Thank you, Your Honor. The defense calls Carl Swartz to the stand."

Swartz hesitated, then looked at Ellen, then lowered his head. After the bailiff swore him in, District attorney Nelson started asking his questions. "Mister Swartz, what's your occupation?"

"I'm an undertaker."

"And where do you live?"

"Five-fifty Shadow Lane, Savannah, Georgia."

"How far is five-fifty Shadow Lane from the Barlow's home?"

"Not far, maybe a few blocks or so."

"Do you know the Barlows?"

"I know them, but only because of my profession."

"Explain that."

"I buried one of their children . . . well not a real child."
"What do you mean by *not a real child?*"

"Well, it was a miscarriage, a miscarriage of a baby not yet fully developed."

"Is it common to bury something like that?"

Bentley took a deep breath and stood up. Your Honor, there's no reason to go into such deep details. The defense accepts that Mister Swartz knows the Barlow family, including young Andrew."

"I agree. Mister Nelson, crack the egg and get to the yolk."

"Yes, Your Honor," Nelson said. "I was only showing the

court that Mister Swartz knew the defendant if he saw him, but if it pleases the court and the defense accepts this, I'll go to what the witness knows about the death of Billy Ricardo."

"Please, Sir, do so," the judge said, followed by a deep sigh and a shake of his head.

Nelson continued. "So, Mister Swartz, you know Andrew Barlow when you see him."

"Yes, sir, I do."

"What about Billy Ricardo?"

"He's dead. What about him?"

Nelson's frustration was evident. "Yes, I know the boy's dead, but did you know him before you saw him die?"

"Yes, sir, I *did* know him when I saw him."

"Tell us when you *last* saw him."

"Well, it was about twelve years ago. I can't say what day it was, but I'm sure it was on Halloween. I was up at the graveyard, you know, checking on the grave of one of my *customers*. I don't know why, but kids play up there a lot, so I didn't think anything about him being there."

"Was he by himself?"

"Yes, at least I didn't see anyone with him."

"What about Andrew Barlow? Did you see him that same day?"

"Yes, I saw him as I was coming back from the cemetery,"

DA Nelson looked at the judge with a smugly smile. "Thank you, Your Honor. I don't have any more questions for this witness."

"I assume the defense wants to cross-examine this witness," the judge said.

"Yes, Your Honor, I do," Bentley said as she ran her hand down her favorite outfit, the one she always wore when she wanted to give the vision of not being too enticing yet appealing enough to get the Judge's attention. Then she started questioning the witness. "Mister Swartz, I see you wear glasses. They look like bifocals."

"Yes, ma'am, they are."

"Do you wear them all the time?"

Swartz took off his glasses and held them up into the light, then readjusted them on his face. "Yes, ma'am, I wear them most of the time."

"Were you wearing them the day you said you saw Andrew go up to the cemetery?"

Swartz bit his lips and lived as he thought about the question. "Hum, I think I did, but," another hum. "You know, I'm not sure if I did or not, Miss Nelson, but I don't need them other than doing my work or reading."

"So you're sure you saw both boys that day?"

"Yes, ma'am, I saw the Ricardo boy while I was up there. He was bouncing around from one stone to another. I started to tell him to stop stomping on the graves, but knowing him, I figured it was best not to say anything."

"So you saw both Billy Swartz and Andrew Barlow playing in the cemetery?"

. "No, not playing. I saw one when I was up there and the other when I came down."

"Now, I want to be sure, Mister Swartz," Bentley said. "You said you saw Billy Ricardo playing in the cemetery, but you didn't see Andrew Barlow in the graveyard with him, is that right?"

Swartz narrowed his brow as he thought about the question. "Yes, ma'am, that's right. I saw the Barlow boy at the path to the cemetery, so I figured he would be going up there. But no, I didn't see the two boys together."

"Thank you, Your Honor," Bentley said. "That's all the questions regarding Billy Ricardo's *accident* we have for Mister Swartz at this time."

McDowell pointed to Nelson. "Cross-examination, Mister District Attorney?"

"Your Honor, the State doesn't have any further questions regarding Mister Ricardo's *suicide* either. So, if it pleases the court, we would like to go to the death of Pastor Garland."

Bentley rose from her seat. "Your Honor, the defense agrees."

McDowell motioned to Nelson, "Call your witness, Mister DA."

"Thank you, Your Honor. The prosecution calls Mrs. Alena Wilson to the stand."

Mrs. Wilson was a long-time widow who worked for the West Side People's Church for almost twenty years. Despite the arrival of another Pastor, a much younger man, she felt lost with Parson Garland gone. She struggled to the stand with a bible in one hand and a walking cane in the other.

"It's good to see you, Mrs. Wilson," Nelson said. "I used to go to your church regularly until I moved away. You didn't have a cane the last time I saw-"

Judge McDowell showed his frustration again. "Counselor, this is a court hearing, not a Bible Study meeting, so please get along with questioning your witness."

"Sorry, Your Honor," Nelson said with a smirk as he turned back to Mrs. Wilson. "Now, Mrs. Wilson, what is your current position?"

"Same as it's been for twenty years or more," Mrs. Wilson replied.

Nelson ignored her smugly tone and continued. "And where would that be?"

Mrs. Wilson wiped away the tear on her cheek with her linen handkerchief. "You know where I work, Mister Nelson. I'm still at Pastor Garland's church."

"Tell the Judge what happened the day the Pastor left to see his brother."

"I remember it well. It was Halloween, and the Pastor was getting ready to go to his brother's house in Pembroke to do a wedding ceremony. Just before he left, the Barlow boy came by."

"Although the boy you saw was in a Halloween costume, you still recognized him?" Nelson asked.

"Of course, I recognized him," Mrs. Wilson said as she

pointed at Andrew. "It's the boy sitting over there. It was him, Andrew Barlow. He was dressed up like a policeman, and he gave the Pastor a box of cookies. He said he made them himself, and it was like a reverse trick or treat."

DA Nelson looked up at McDowell and smiled. "That's all the State has with this witness, Your Honor."

"The witness is yours for cross-examination, counselor," McDowell said as he fiddled with some papers on his desk.

Bentley uncrossed her long legs and approached Mrs. Wilson. "I'm I'm sorry for your loss, Mrs. Wilson," she said as she approached the witness. "A lot of people will miss him."

Mrs. Wilson wiggled in her seat, sniffled, and nodded. "He was a good man."

"I'm sure he was, Mrs. Wilson, but what I want to ask you about now is did-" She hesitated as she looked at Andrew. "Did that thirteen-year-old boy sitting over there givePastor Garland poisoned cookies??"

Mrs. Wilson wiped tears from her cheek, looked at Andrew, then back at Bentley. "I didn't know they were poisoned."

"What made you think they were poisoned later?"

"Well, I guess it was when the Police told me, or maybe it was Mister Nelson. I just can't remember."

"Was the Pastor there at that time?"

"Yes, he was, but-"

"Did you see Pastor Garland eat any of the cookies?"

"Well, no, ma'am, I didn't see him, but knowing how the Pastor likes . . . liked . . . sweets, I figured he would."

"So you didn't actually see him eating any of the cookies?" Bentley repeated in her calming tone.

"Well . . . I guess I didn't," Mrs. Wilson said."But about thirty minutes after the Pastor left, he called me to tell me he was feeling sick and was coming back home."

"Did he say it was the cookies that made him sick." it?" Bentley asked.

"He might have, but I was so worried, I'm not sure."

"Then all you can testify is that the Pastor took the cookies with him, not that he ate anyone of them?"

"I guess all I know for sure is that he just said he was sick and was coming back home."

"Did you tell anyone else about that?"

Mrs. Wilson stuttered as she pointed to Detectives Marten and Bradley. "I mentioned it to those two detectives over there when they came by asking about him. I remember they asked me about the cookies and if Pastor Garland ate any of them." Mrs. Wilson said as she wiped more tears from her face. "I told them the same I told you, Pastor Garland liked sweets, so I'd be surprised if he didn't."

"Just to make it clear, Mrs. Wilson, you testified that you *thought* Pastor Garland may have eaten the *alleged* poisoned cookies? Is that right?"

"Yes-I mean, no, I never asked him."

"So, you didn't see him eat them?" Bentley repeated. "You just thought he *might* have eaten them. Is that right?"

Another nod, followed by more sniffles and more tears.

DA Nelson was quick to stand up. "Your Honor, what difference does it make if the witness asked about cookies or if he ever brought them up? We do have proof that they were poisoned. With *symptoms* of a heart attack, thinking about cookies may not have been on the Pastor's mind."

"Sit down, counselor," McDowell said as he glared at Bentley. "The prosecution makes a good point, counselor. What difference does it make?"

Bentley gave the Judge an alluring smile as she answered his question. "The prosecution attorney is right, Your Honor. If you're in the middle of a heart attack, as the Pembroke coroner said Pastor Garland was, you're not likely to be thinking about a box of cookies."

Nelson was on his feet again. "Your Honor, the prosecution was not validating a heart attack as the reason-"

The judge took the opportunity to embarrass his opponent. "Sit down, counselor," McDowell grumbled. "You opened that box." After a minute of thought, he nodded to Bentley. "The witness may answer that."

Mrs. Wilson seemed confused. "I'm not sure. Knowing he was feeling bad upset me. Then the phone call in the middle night from the Pembroke police telling me he was dead, just-" Tears were building up again. "I'm just not sure of anything anymore. All I know is that Pastor Garland never came back."

Seeing Mrs. Wilson's turmoil and believing her responses didn't help the prosecution's argument, Bentley whispered, "Thank you, Mrs. Wilson," she said as she looked up at the judge. "Your Honor, the defense doesn't have any more questions for this witness."

"Thank you, Mrs. Wilson. Again, I'm sorry for your loss and the many in his church." Judge McDowell motioned the two attorneys to come to his bench as he looked at his watch. "If there aren't any more witnesses at this time, we'll recess until Monday at ten o'clock. We'll take up the David Ricardo death then."

Both attorneys agreed.

After adjournment, Nelson met Bentley outside of the courtroom. "Maria, we need to bring this hearing to a close," he said. "All you have to do is to accept a guilty plea. I'll agree to Andrew's detention in a juvenile center until he's eighteen if you do. Otherwise, I'll go for a Class A felony. That puts him in the big house for most of his life."

Bentley laughed. "Earl, you must see an acquittal coming, or you would never make a concession, and from what I hear, you are losing. I know the Barlows' answer, but I'll pass your *goodwill* offer to them. Now, if you want to make a real offer, drop David Ricardo's *suicide*."

"The offer is only good for Billy Ricardo's and Pastor

Garland's deaths," Nelson said with a smirk. "David Ricardo is another issue."

"If you don't do any better, Earl, that one will slip out of your hands too."

"You won't be so sure about that when we get to his murder on Monday?"

"Guess we'll just have to see, Earl," Bentley said with a smile as she led the Barlows into a back room. However, the smile didn't cover the tense look on her face.

Ellen was upset; Michael was angry; Andrew was indifferent. Michael put his arm around Ellen. "It's going to be okay, honey," he promised, then looked at his attorney. How do you think it's going?"

"Well, the prosecution seems to think it's not going well for them. I think Nelson regrets bringing Mrs. Wilson in as a witness. She helped us a lot more than she helped him. That might be why he made his offer."

"What offer?" Michael asked.

"It wasn't a great offer," Bentley said, "but it might keep Andrew out of prison-if he was found guilty. But knowing how you and Mrs. Barlow feel about anything other than sending him home, I turned him down. But you might think about it."

"No!" Ellen shouted. "Never! I'll never let them put my son in prison."

Andrew seemed to wake up when he heard the adult conversation. "Why don't you just tell them I didn't do it?"

"It doesn't work that way, Andrew," Bentley said. "But don't you worry. We get to bring in witnesses later today that'll show you're innocent. But for now, we need to get you some lunch, ok?"

*   *   *

An hour later, Judge McDowell called the court back into session.

DA Nelson stood up. "Your honor, the State calls the county Medical Examiner, Doctor Louis Redman, to the stand."

Doctor Redman took his place on the witness stand. After the bailiff swore him in, Attorney General Nelson began his questioning. "Doctor, please tell the court what your current position is."

"I'm the County Medical Examiner."

"And how long have you been in that position."

"How long totally or how long have I been in Georgia?"

"Both would be acceptable, so-"

Attorney Bentley interrupted Redman. "Your Honor, the defense accepts Doctor Redman's credentials."

"Accepted," McDowell said as he pointed at Nelson. "The AD can go ahead with his questioning."

The questioning went through David Ricardo's postmortem performed by Doctor Larson. "I'm not criticizing the previous Medical Examiners competence, but-"

Nelson interrupted Redman. "Then what made you look at his postmortem file?"

"The Detective over there," Redman said as he pointed to Marten. "She was reviewing several deaths, and David Ramirez happened to be one of them. When she asked me to look at deaths in the area again, I agreed to do that. I started with the Ricardo file."

"Did you find anything different than what Doctor Larson found when he first saw Ricardo's body?"

"Doctor Larson did an excellent job of doing all of his investigations. But in this case, he had the body in front of him. That was more of an advantage than the photos I had to look at, so he shouldn't have missed anything."

"Did you find anything in the photos?" Anything the previous Examiner might have missed?"

"As I said, I'm not criticizing the previous Medical Examiners competence, but he did miss something."

"And what was that?"

"A small but important detail," Redman said as he pulled several photos out of his file and held up one of David Ricardo's body. "Just a quick look at a body, especially one already decided to be a suicide," Redman continued, "it's easy to miss some details. Unfortunately, that's what Doctor Larson did."

"And what did he miss?"

"What he missed was the angle of the bullet going into the deceased's head."

"Just a minute, Doctor, come over here and use the blow-up photo so we all can see what you found." Nelson handed Redman a wooden wand as he came in front of the stand holding a blow-up photo, then he pointed to the lines drawn up and down on the head of the deceased David Ricardo. "Point out to the Judge what you saw that your predecessor did not see."

"The angle here," Redman said as he moved his wand up and down. "It shows the angle the bullet took when it hit the deceased's head. In most gun suicides, the shot is at the side of the head, close to the ear. Not always, though. Sometimes they shoot into the forehead, as did this one, but if this were a suicide, the angle would have traveled on one of these angles," he said as he trailed the lines on the photos with his finger up the face. "But this pullet went at a level angle directly *into* the deceased's forehead and into the brain."

Nelson handed him a wooden gun mimicking the gun that shot Ricardo. Redman held the fake gun at different places in the head. "You can see what I mean."

Nelson took the gun back, turned to the judge, and returned to Redman. "So, as a professional Medical Examiner, your opinion is that someone, someone other than Mister Ricardo, had to point the gun directly at his forehead and pull the trigger?"

"Yes, sir. I based my opinion on the angle the bullet took going into the deceased head," he said as he pointed the photo and traced a trail leading to the bullet hole. It's difficult for anyone to shoot himself in this area. In fact, it would be almost impossible."

"Then, in your opinion, this was a murder, not a suicide?"

"Yes, sir, this was a murder, not a suicide."

"Did you find anything else, Doctor?"

"That's all I found, but the forensic department found something else."

"And what was that, sir?"

"The only other fingerprints on the gun, besides David Ricardo's, was that of Andrew Barlow."

Nelson looked at Bentley, then back at the judge. "Your Honor, the prosecution rests."

The judge hammered his gavel as he tried to quiet the flush of mumbling that suddenly filled the gallery. "Quiet, or I'll empty this courtroom," he shouted as his gavel hit the bench again. Once the noise faded, he nodded to Miss Bentley. "Is the defendant ready for your rebuttal? If so, you're up now."

"Your Honor, can we have a brief recess while I have a conversation with my client?"

McDowell nodded. "That, ma'am, would be a good idea."

Both Ellen and Michael were speechless. "What just happened?" Michael asked.

"Mister Barlow, all I know is that suddenly things aren't going as good as we thought. Let me talk to the prosecutor, and I'll get right back to you."

Earl Nelson was in his office when Maria Bentley pushed

open his door. "Whatever became of knocking?" he said with a grin on his face. It was clear to Bentley he knew he had won. The only question left was what he would offer if anything.

"Okay, Earl, Redman's testimony hurt our case, but it did not kill it."

"Then why did you come rushing into my office?"

Bentley ignored his question. "I know the evidence is now in your favor, so I want to know if there's anything we can agree on when we go back to the Judge."

"All I will agree on now will be charging the boy as an adult."

"Be serious, Earl," Bentley shouted. "You know Andrew doesn't deserve years in prison, if not all of his years, and you know I'll never accept that. Even if I did, the Barlow's would never accept it, and I don't think the judge would either."

"You want to gamble on that.'

Maria took a deep breath and shook her head. "Earl, he's just thirteen, just a boy."

"What do you want to put on the table, Maria?"

"Not guilty! Not guilty due to insanity!" Bentley waited for Earl's response. "Come on, Earl! Pleading insanity will put him away in some asylum for the rest of his teenage years. More important for you, it would show your compassion. That can't hurt you in the polls."

"Hmm," Nelson mumbled as he left Bentley waiting for an answer, then he said, "Not guilty due to insanity? That might be something I could agree on, but only if you can find a psychiatrist that will diagnose him as being insane."

Bentley only took a few minutes to go back to the Barlows. The sad look on her face was telling as she explained the agreement Nelson agreed to. "But only if you agree."

Ellen looked at Michael, then back at the attorney. "Do you think he's insane?"

"It doesn't matter what I think or what you think. Our case fell apart with the Medical Examiner's testimony that Andrew was present when David Ricardo died and his fingerprints being on the gun. If the judge decides to treat Andrew as an adult, the State will eventually look into the deaths of Mrs. Collin and Billy Ricardo again. If that happens, I have no doubt Andrew would end up in prison for many years."

Ellen buried her face in her hands then shouted, "God, help me, I don't know what to do."

Michael grabbed her hand. "Honey, I don't believe our son is insane, and I'll never believe he killed anyone, but our options are limited. Remember, Doctor Ramirez was concerned about what he heard during his sessions with Andrew, the pictures he drew, and what he said in his hypnosis session. If our son has some mental issues, he would be better off in an asylum-just long enough for them to deal with whatever problems he has. At least it will keep him out of years in prison."

Bentley had a surprised look on her face. "Andrew's been seeing a psychiatrist? Why didn't you tell me this before?"

"I think he was a psychologist," Michael said. "We started to tell you, but Ellen was afraid it would make him look like a crazy boy when he was just a confused boy."

"This might sound strange, Mister Barlow, but that just might be what we need to convince the judge that a psychiatrist's opinion would be enough to justify keeping Andrew in Youth Detention instead of prison. I'll ask the judge and the prosecuting attorney to meet with us."

CHAPTER XVII

W<small>HILE</small> M<small>ARIA</small> B<small>ENTLEY</small> <small>WAS</small> <small>DISCUSSING</small> <small>WHICH</small> psychiatric facility would be best for Andrew, Andrew was back at the Center under the supervision of Mrs. Willard. After Freddy's injury, most other residents stayed away from Andrew. Except for meals, he spent his days and night isolated in his room. Even then, all he got from the others were whispers and caustic glares from one table to another. Gradually, he became more and more withdrawn. As he seemed to fade away, Jimm became more and more in control.

> *Some of them are jealous because you got me*
> *for a friend and others are just afraid of us.*
> *They're the smart ones.*

"I don't care 'about them, and I don't care about you," Andrew said as tears ran down his pale face. "I miss my mom and dad."

You don't need nobody but me.

"It's you that gets me in all this trouble, trouble like what happened to Freddy. He didn't just fall, he was pushed, and I didn't do it. I wanted him to be my friend. But you-you don't want me to have any friends 'cept you!"

Fatty boy was going to hurt you. I was just taking care of you like I always do. Anyway, we're in this together, so we gotta stick together. Besides, they gonna let us out of here after you talk to that doctor.

"What if she don't let me go home?"

She will if you let me do the talkin'.

"No, you'll just scare her."

Scarring her might help, but she might think I'm a bit crazy. So maybe it might be best that you do the talkin'.

*   *   *

The following afternoon, forty-year-old Child Psychiatrist Doctor Marsha Brown met with Andrew, Ellen, Michael, and Maria Bentley. After adjusting her blonde hair curled around her head, she put on her bifocal glasses. "So you're the young man I hear so much about," she asked as she shook Andrew's hand.

"Yes, ma'am, I'm Andrew."

"Since we're going to spend a lot of time together, is it okay if I call you Andy?" she asked.

Andrew hesitated for a minute, then surprisingly to his parents, he said, "Yes, ma'am. I like Andy."

"Great," Doctor Brown said as she smiled at Ellen. Mrs. Barlow, you, your husband, and Miss Bentley can let me and Andy get to know each other. You can come back in an hour or so." After they were alone, Doctor Brown sat Andrew down on a leather couch.

"Do you want me to lay down, Doctor Brown?"

"If that's what you want to do, Andy."

"I saw a movie once where a man was seeing a crazy doctor, and he had to lay down."

Doctor Brown laughed. "Well, Andy, that's just a movie, and I'm not really a *crazy Doctor*. I'm what they call a psychiatrist."

"Are you going to give me medicine?"

"Do you think you need medicine?"

"The lady at the Center said I needed some, but I don't need any medicine 'cause I'm not sick."

"Well, you know there are a lot of different types of sickness. Some need medicine; some just need what I call *talking medicine*. So we're going to just talk for a while."

After a half-hour of conversation about school, friends, what he liked, and what he didn't like, Doctor Brown eased into a more personal conversation. "Andrew, your parents told me you had a brother. Can you tell me about him?"

Andrew began to breathe deeply. "I don't know much about that."

"Sometimes, people know things that they don't want others to know they know. Do you know why?"

Andrew shook his head. "No, ma'am, I don't know why."

"Well, they think other people will think they're weird or crazy. Do you ever feel that people might think that about you?"

"I'm not crazy or anything, but I might do things I shouldn't do."

"Tell me about it, Andy. I promise I won't think you're crazy. In fact, I think you're a very smart boy."

Don't! Don't listen to her. She's trying to trick you.

"She won't. I like her!"

Ignoring the third party, Doctor Brown smiled. "I'm glad you like me, Andrew. I think we're going to get along very well."

Doctor Brown took advantage of the gentility of her patient. It was time to open the door where the other party lived. "Who were you talking to, Andy?" she asked. "Your brother?"

Although her question was free of astonishment and condemnation, it caught Andrew off guard. "I was just saying-"

Shut up! You're sayin' too much!

"No! I won't shut up. You keep doing bad things, and you need to stop!" Then he looked up at Doctor Brown. "Sorry, ma'am. Sometimes I just talk to myself."

With the door open, all she had to do was to step through it. "Or somebody?" she asked in a nonjudgmental tone. However, Andrew still backed away.

Andrew shook his head. "Maybe, sometimes, but not a lot."

Doctor Brown responded with a smile that said, *'everything will be okay.'*

> *Careful! Don't let that fake smile fool you. She's*
> *just trying to set you up.*

Andrew ignored the voice.

"That's okay, Andrew," Brown continued. "I've met a lot of people who do that. Sometimes another person, an invisible person to others but real to the person, might understand what you worry about." After minutes of quietness, Brown continued. "But you are in control, so push this *person* away and talk to me."

Andrew was puzzled. No one else had ever understood what was going on in his mind. "You believe me?"

"Let's just say I believe that you believe, Andy."

An hour later, Andrew finished with, "So, sometimes he does things, bad things, things I don't like, and I get blamed for them. But he's my brother, so I let him."

"Andy, was it *Him* that killed Mister Ricardo and his son?"

"I don't know. We weren't talkin' to each other much then, but *He* could have."

"What about the cookies you gave to Pastor Garland and Mrs. Jackson?"

"I just gave them the cookies, but *He* made them."

Doctor Brown took a deep breath as she put her arms around Andrew. "What's his name, Andy?"

Andrew covered his face with his hand and began crying again. "He said his name is *Jimm!*"

*　　*　　*

"It's like a Jekyll and Hyde story, Your Honor," Doctor Brown said as she addressed Judge McDowell in closed session. "His brother is real to him. Unfortunately, I don't know of anything that can change that."

"And your opinion on where he should go?"

"Not in prison for sure, Your Honor," she said. "He would be a helpless victim there. I suggest you place him in a state psychiatrist facility. I have patients in Georgia's State Mental Asylum in Milledgeville where I can follow him."

"I thought you said there was no help for him."

"What I meant, Your Honor, is there are no medicines that will cure him, at least none that I know about. However, with my colleagues and me working with him, over time, *Mister Hyde* might fade away."

CHAPTER XVIII

ELLEN AND MICHAEL VISITED ANDREW AT GEORGIA'S State Mental Asylum twice a month and always on his birthday. This visit, however, she came alone. After checking in, she asked to see Andrew's doctor before seeing her son.

"Doctor Brown's office is her way," the nurse said as she led Ellen down the dark hall.

"How is Andrew doing," Ellen asked. Her tone was somber.

"He seems to be doing better, Mrs. Barlow. No fights and only a few episodes of talking to his invisible friend." A wide smile followed. "But, he does argue with Mister Pinocchio now and then, but even then, it seems to be a one-way conversation."

"He's done that since his father gave it to him on one of his birthdays."

"That's not unusual. I see a lot of it. In fact, it seems to be beneficial; you know, having someone to tell your secrets to, knowing they'll keep them. Bye the way, where is Mister Barlow?"

"He's not coming."

"Andrew will be disappointed," the nurse said as she pointed to a small couch. "Make yourself comfortable.

Doctor Brown is making her rounds now, but she'll be here soon."

When Brown arrived, she saw a solemn-looking Ellen Barlow. "I'd ask how are you doing, but I see you're not doing well. I also see that Mister Barlow isn't here. Is he still sick?"

Ellen responded with a sudden flow of tears. Doctor Brown handed her a tissue from his desk as he sat next to her. "My husband is dead, Doctor," Ellen said as she wiped tears from her face. "He had what they call Black Lung disease from working in the coal mines up in Ohio for a long time. He fought it for the last few months, then two days ago, he lost the battle."

"I'm so sorry, Mrs. Barlow, Doctor Brown said as she took her by the hand. " He was a good man, and Andrew loved him a lot."

"Yes, he did. That's what I want to talk to you about, Doctor. I want him to come home for the funeral tomorrow. If he doesn't, he'll never forgive me."

* * *

They buried Michael Barlow next to his son, Jimm. Ellen was surprised over how calm Andrew took his father's death. After the funeral, all he had to say was, "Why did Dad die, Mommy?"

"He was sick for a long time, Andrew."

"So it wasn't because of *Him*?" Andrew asked as he pointed to Jimm Barlow II's tombstone.

Either Ellen didn't hear her son, or knowing she had enough things to worry about already, she ignored him. Life without Michael was more than she could handle, much less having to deal with her son's imaginary brother. Maya heard him, however. It brought a stunning look to her face. *Oh, my God, not again*, fluttered in her mind."

As they left the cemetery, Andrew became more agitated. "Are you going to be okay, Andrew?" Maya asked.

Welcome home, Brother.

"Thanks to you, I can't stay, so leave me alone."

Ellen heard him. "Andrew, as much as Mrs. Jackson's done for you and me, that's no way to talk to her!"

Maya put her arm around Ellen and whispered, "It's okay, Ellen. I don't think he was talking to me."

"Then to who?"

Maya hesitated to answer.

Ellen and Maya went into the kitchen while Andrew went up to the attic when they arrived at the house. Soon, they heard him talking to himself or someone else.

"NO! Not that again," Ellen muttered s the attic sounds floated down into the kitchen. "I can't go through his imagination again."

"Ellen, this might sound weird, but I don't think it's his imagination."

Ellen gave Maya a puzzled look. "If not that, then is he just crazy?"

"I don't think he's crazy, and I don't think he's making

his *friend* up. He was doing good at the asylum without medicines, but as soon as he came back to this house, things started back as they had been over the past years." Maya waited for Ellen to respond, but all she heard was a deep sigh and a frightened look.

"Call it my Jamaica history, but I believe there is more to it than his imagination. I think it's this house."

Ellen shook her head and began crying again. "Whatever it is, I can't go through it anymore, at least not now."

"I understand," Maya said as she looked up the steps to the attic. "It's best we get him back to the Asylum as soon as we can."

CHAPTER XIX

It was Halloween and Andrew's eighteenth birthday when they discharged him from the State Mental Asylum. He was welcomed back to the house on 666 Shadow Lane by a blistering storm.

Shadow Lane had changed over the four years he was away. Shortly after his father died from breast cancer, his mother died—another grave with a Barlow tombstone in the cemetery.

When Randy Jackson's PTSD worsened, he committed suicide, leaving Maya to move back to Jamaica. Over time, the path to the cemetery was overgrown. Gradually, tall weeds found their way into the graveyard, hiding the stones themselves. Over time, the Ricardo house became victim to the wind and rain. Finally, age won and demolished the house.

Despite heavy winter storms and smothering hot summers, the house on 666 Shadow Lane and its leafless trees still stood.

The storm was coming in from the east, bringing howling winds that made the bare branches of tortured trees shiver. Shudders banged against windows they were meant to protect until they too became victims and jerked free of their hinges, allowing the porch swing to take out its anger on the unprotected window. In turn, the window sent slivers of glass flying into the creaking house. However, Andrew was not concerned about heavy winds and shattered glass.

He tried to open the houses' door. It remained closed. He tried again; this time, the door rewarded him with a grating sound as the hinges gave way. Slowly the door opened. Once inside the house, he ran his fingers across the wall, searching for the light switch. Once he found one, it was useless. The house remained dark.

In the shack behind the house, he found two kerosene lanterns. He lit them and took them to the house. Their fluttering flame only increased the sarcastic vision of the dimness in the dungy living room. Dancing flames from crackling logs in the fireplace only added to the house's seed of despondence.

Knees crossed, Andrew sat in front of the fireplace. Although he did not need the warmth, the flickering flames gave him as much comfort as the extent the *House* would allow. He ran his hands through his shaggy hair as he took himself back to all the years he had blamed the house for replacing his life's comfort, comfort that most children had for just being a boy, with whispers and torments. His worse memory was not being free to be the boy he wanted to be.

His eyes scanned the room as he searched for memories of the past. The steps leading to the attic were the first thing that caught his eyes. Although his memories were faint, he remembered who had ruined his life, who had separated him from his father and mother, and who had him put away from the real world for years. In his eyes, his past fantasies were no longer specters. He was no longer *Him*. He was now Andrew Barlow again. Rattling from the attic, then. *THUMP, THUMP, THUMP.*

The familiar footsteps coming down the squeaking steps brought him back to the present. Then the voice:

> *You're still living in a fantasy world if you think you've gotten stronger, Brother, but it's the House. It's alive, and it has been alive ever since it was host to its double murder years ago. It's strong. It has always been strong, but it's grown even stronger over the years! It held me here, knowing you would come back.*

"NO! It's just a house! It's you that doesn't exist. You never existed. You're not my brother. You're just a fantasy. This house is just a run-down pile of wood. Do you hear me? You're not my bother! My brother is buried in the cemetery."

As his words echoed throughout the house, the walls shuddered. A burst of fire from the open fireplace followed. As his eyes closed, his head began shaking, and his shouts turned into screams while hard fists slammed into his forehead.

> *Don't blame me, Brother. Both of us were born here, here in this house, the only house we've*

ever known. Without the House, I would not
be here. I would still be rotting in a jar. No, it
ain't me, Brother. It's the House.

Andrew realized Jimm was right; the *House* was behind everything.

I was angry when I saw that old, grey-haired
woman pull you out then push me into a pan
of water. But the House wouldn't let it separate
us. It thrived on us. Eventually, we needed it
as much as it needed us, but it took eight years
before it could reach out to me. Like it has for
years, it gave me existence enough to reach out
to you.

The years he had been held captive by guilt and fear, years of taking the blame for things he didn't do, years of lying to keep a secret that he couldn't explain, and years of not having a life of his own flooded through Andrew's mind. "No! This has got to stop!" he shouted. "You've all ways pushed me aside, but no more! I won't be your or the *House's* captive any longer! This has to end! This will end!"

There's no end, Brother. The House won't
let it end, and I won't let it end as long as I
remember how our parents loved you, loved

you while I was struggling to be part of the family. It was always, you, always Andrew.

"They loved you even when there was no *You*," Andrew replied. "They gave you a name, they gave you a funeral, they buried you even when there was nothing to bury. And what did you give them other than horror and sadness? It was me who smothered you in her womb, not Mom. It was me who used you to bring me into the world. If you want to blame anyone, blame me."

You are to blame, brother. It was you who took my life away before I even had one.

"And how many lives did you take away in your greed, selfishness, and anger?" Andrew shouted. "I'll tell you how many! Mrs. Collins, when you pushed her down the attic steps after killing her cat, Billy Ricardo when you smashed his head against a tombstone, his father when you pulled the trigger sending a bullet into his head, feeding rat poison to Pastor Garland, and overdosing Maya Jackson's insulin. The old undertaker would be on your list if they hadn't put us away. Add to this the innocent boy you killed when we were in the crazy house. You even wanted to kill my parents, but I kept you away from them until they died normal deaths."

They were our parents! Our parents! But they only wanted you, so they shoved me into a glass jar as if I didn't exist. But you have a share of the blame too, Brother. I wouldn't have; I couldn't have done anything without you.

"I wanted to stop you, but I couldn't."

You saved our parents, and you could have saved the rest, but you didn't. Instead, you stood by and let me do what you couldn't do. Their blood is on your hands.

"On hands you controlled. But yes, I take the blame for not stopping you in the beginning. If I could change things, I would, but I can't. All I can do is to put you to rest."

We might have separate minds, brother. Other than that, we're the same. You can't do anything. You can't separate us. You can't get rid of me. I'm part of you, and we're both a part of the House.

Andrew stood up, walked away from the fireplace, and grabbed one of the emergency lamps. "You're wrong, Jimm. There is a way to put you at rest! A way to put both of us at rest!"

The House's began to shiver, making shattered curtains quiver against broken glass.

Brother, don't! We can still be together. I can
change. We can keep being brothers. Please-

"If you could change, Jimm, why didn't you?" Before
the voice could answer, Andrew threw the lantern against
the room, splattering kerosene into the fireplace. Within
seconds, the flame spread from the fireplace across the
room. Window curtains caught fire, then the wall. As the
fire blazed, Andrew sat back down in front of the fireplace.
"We'll be together, Jimm. For once, we will be together.
That's what you wanted, isn't it?"

*   *   *

The fire truck arrived just in time to save most of the
house but not soon enough to save the young man inside.
Carl Swartz buried the remains of Andrew Barlow next to
his brother Jimm, his mother, and his father in the graveyard
behind 666 Shadow Lane

Nolan Walter and his wife, Betty, and their son, Daniel,
left New Jersey to go to Savannah, Georgia, and open a new
restaurant. Their first stop was at Mary Ann's real estate
agency.

"Welcome to Savannah, folks," Mary Ann said when
they arrived. "I like to think about this part of Savannah as
being more like a town than a city."

"That fits us just fine," Betty said. "We're looking for a
quiet place and a house within our budget."

Mary Ann smiled as she walked them to her car. "I think I can help you with that. Now the house I'm going to show you had a lot of fire damage a year or so ago, but it's been repaired and looks as good as it was when it was new." Twenty minutes later, she made a left turn. "This is Shadow Lane."

"A funny name," Nolan said.

"Yes, it is," Mary Ann said with a smile. See all of those tall oak trees? It was named after the shade they get from them. You know, no sun, no shadows," she said with a laugh. "It's been on the market for a while, so I'm sure I can get the price to fit your budget."

"Look at the big trees, Nolan," Betty said as they turned into 999 Shadow Lane. "It's just like she said it would be."

"You might think it's wonderful, but I'll have to rake up all those leaves when they start falling in the fall. Other than that, the place looks like it was just built."

"Go on and look inside," Mary Ann said. "It's unlocked and ready for you to move in."

"Go ahead, Betty," Nolan said. "I need to get my camera out of the car."

"You're a picture, man, I see," Mary Ann said after Betty left.

"Kind of a hobby thing. Betty gets irritated sometimes, you know, a picture of this, a picture of that. Anyway, I want to send photos of the house back to folks in Jersey. Seeing this house at this price might urge them to move down here too."

As Nolan headed to the house, Mary Ann stopped. "Now

that we're alone, Mister Walter, there's something I should tell you about the house you're moving into." Whispering, she continued. "I was asked not to tell you about it, but since you'll be living there, I think you need to know."

"Should I be scared?" Nolan asked.

Mary Ann hesitated to answer, then she smiled. "No, it's nothing of importance. Just that there's a cemetery behind your house, other than that, I think you'll like the house."

"A graveyard? Betty will love that. It'll make Halloween that much more spooky."

Mary Ann closed her eyes, sighed, and smiled in relief. "I'll be the first knocking on your door next Halloween, Mister Walter." As they entered the house, she turned the drooping house numbers around.

THE END